GREETINGS!

MY NAME IS B.O.R.T.R.O.N. AND FOR CENTURIES MY CREWS AND I HAVE TRAVELED THE GLOBE TO SAVE LIVES AND PROPERTY.

SOME PEOPLE THINK I'M A SPACESHIP, BUT ACTUALLY I AM AN ACCELERATED SPACE AND DISTANCE (ASD) TRANSPORTER. WHAT DOES THAT MEAN?, YOU MAY BE WONDERING. WELL, IF YOU CAN IMAGINE TRAVELING TO THE OTHER SIDE OF THE WORLD IN THE BLINK OF AN EYE AND ENTERING AN ALTERED TIME ZONE THAT ALLOWS YOU TO ACCOMPLISH ASTONISHING THINGS IN THE EQUIVALENT OF MINUTES AT HOME, THEN YOU'VE GOT IT!

ON THIS MISSION TO ITALY, THE CLUB US CREW MUST STOP THE MELTDOWN OF VEHICLES THROUGHOUT THE COUNTRY ON THE SAME DAY, AT THE SAME TIME, AND SAVE MILLIONS OF LIVES. IT'S A THRILL A MINUTE, AND YOU CAN BE A PART OF IT BY JUST TURNING THE PAGE.

BUCKLE UP AND GET READY FOR THE RIDE OF YOUR LIFE!

CLUB US
by Mya Reyes

Published by ValMar Publishing
Las Vegas, NV 89145 USA

www.ValMarPublishing.com

© 2021 Mya Reyes
All rights reserved. No portion of this book may be reproduced in any form without permission from the publisher, except as permitted by U.S. copyright law.

For permissions contact:
info@ValMarPublishing.com

Cover illustration by Claudia Gadotti
Graphics by Kate Z. Stone & Jake Naylor

ISBN: 978-1-955079-03-7

Intrigue in Italy

Mya Reyes

Cover illustration by Claudia Gadotti
Graphics by Kate Z. Stone and Jake Naylor

VALMAR
PUBLISHING

Here's what they're saying!

"This is the third CLUB US book I've read and it was so much fun! My mom is Italian, and she liked hearing me talk about their adventures. Now I'm really excited to go to Italy again on family vacation."
— Davide, age 11

"I like reading the CLUB US books because the kids are always getting into trouble and they always figure out a way to make it work. Eddie is my favorite."
— Cindi, age 9

"Ciao! I like reading the CLUB US books because the kids are having an adventure and learning another language too."
— Lionel, age 12

"I read Peril in Paris and Crisis in Cuba and they were both funny and exciting. My mom also signed me up as a member in the club on the website. I love my CLUB US T-shirt and passport."
— Sam, age 10

"These books are really awesome for my two kids, ages 9 and 13. I was surprised they both liked them! The stories offer everything they love and they pretended they were on the mission and tried to find answers to the dilemmas the crew members got into. Bravo!"
— Virginia Banuelo, Mom

*To all the kids who will make our world
a better place to live.*

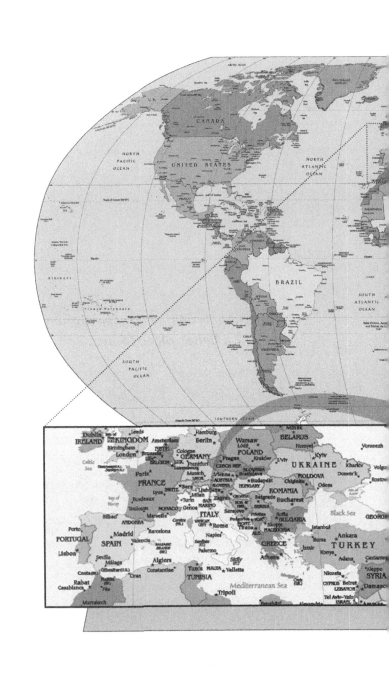

FUN FACTS ABOUT ITALY:

- Italy is shaped like a high-heeled boot.
- Italians eat pasta every day and usually with a different preparation.
- Pizza was invented in Italy.
- Mickey Mouse is called Topolino in Italy, and Goofy is Pippo.
- In Italy, 13 is a lucky number.

YOU CAN JOIN CLUB US!

IT'S FREE!

AS A MEMBER YOU WILL HAVE ACCESS TO DOWNLOAD OR RECEIVE:

- A VIP Membership card
- A CLUB US Passport
- Printable country stamps to add to your passport
- Entry into fun contests
- Newsletters with CLUB US updates and activities
- Access to printables and games
- A sneak peek at upcoming books in the Club Us series

It's easy! Just ask your parent to visit www.clubus.us with you to learn more and sign up!

OUR TEAM

GOLD

NIKKO

KIAN

CASSIE

EDDIE

MR. SMITH

BARKS

Intrigue in Italy

CHAPTER 1
(Uno)

~ oo-noh ~

"Wake up, Mr. Khan. Your limousine is waiting to take you to the theater! Wake up, Mr. Khan. Your limousine is waiting to take you to the theater! Wake up, Mr. Khan. . ."

Kian hit the snooze button. Even though he hated hearing the alarm in the morning, he loved the message it kept repeating. After all, he would soon be a famous magician, with his name in lights on the Las Vegas Strip. The fact that he was still only in sixth grade didn't mean anything at all. It was just a matter of time.

He sat on the side of the bed and started thinking about his next trick. It would be fabulous and no one, not one person, would be able to guess how he did it. He couldn't wait.

Suddenly, he returned to reality and remembered he had to be at Mr. Smith's house, with the rest of the CLUB US crew, at eight o'clock. The clock said seven-thirty. He had thirty minutes to get dressed, grab something to eat, and run down the street to their meeting place. He opened the closet to reveal a row of crisp, white T-shirts. White T-shirts were Kian's trademark. He wore one every day. Whether it was to school, to shop with his mom, or to church on Sunday, his wardrobe didn't change. He didn't have to think about it. Like every morning, he reached in and grabbed one of about thirty choices, pulled on a pair of jeans and shoes, and hurried into the bathroom to brush his teeth and wash his face.

Within minutes, he was running down the stairs to grab something to eat. He looked around the small, white kitchen and didn't see his mom, nor breakfast, anywhere. The one thing he knew would be on the left side of the kitchen table every morning was his dad, reading the *Shanghai Daily* newspaper. It was his way of staying in touch with what was going on in his boyhood city.

"Morning, Dad," said Kian.

"Good morning, my son."

Kian glanced out the kitchen window to see his mom, totally immersed in her Tai Chi exercises. He never understood why she insisted on spending an hour each morning contorting her body into weird poses, but she insisted it made her healthy. He had learned it was easier to go along with the program than to tell her the gym on Woodward Avenue worked just as well, if not better, and she could listen to rock music at the same time.

"Son, what are you doing up so early? There's

no school today," said Mrs. Khan as she walked in the back door and washed her hands at the sink.

"I know, Mom. I'm going to Mr. Smith's house."

She glanced at the clock on the wall. "At this hour? You haven't even eaten breakfast."

"Don't worry," Kian said, opening the door to the refrigerator. "I'll just grab a couple of dumplings left over from last night."

"But they're cold!" protested Mrs. Khan.

She barely finished her sentence before she saw her son run out the front door and head down the street.

"What is wrong with that boy?" she asked her husband as he sipped his green bean coffee. Dr. Khan liked to relax in the mornings before doing his hospital rounds, but his wife always interrupted his tranquility with lots of questions. She generally wanted to know why their son didn't want to become a neurosurgeon like him, when was he going to realize that it was a much better occupation than a magician, and what was his reasoning to wear a white T-shirt every single day.

"Who knows?" answered her husband while turning to the business section of the paper. He had long given up trying to understand his only son, and always had a hard time discussing the boy's behavior with his wife and his family in China.

As Kian passed Cassie's house, the front door opened and his friend walked slowly down the steps to join him.

"Hey Cassie, how ya doing?" asked Kian.

"I'm sleepy. It's crazy to get up so early on spring break. I don't even know if I want to go on this mission. I'm still tired from yesterday," she lamented as they crossed the street to join Gold and Eddie. Like Cassie, they looked like they needed more sleep. Even Eddie's dog, Barks, was walking slower than usual.

When the kids returned from their Cuba

mission yesterday afternoon, they hadn't even had a chance to share their exciting adventure with Mr. Smith before B.O.R.T.R.O.N. informed them they would be going to Italy today.

"I can't believe we're going on another mission," said Eddie, rubbing his eyes, but still full of excitement. "I can't wait."

"Eddie, you're crazy," said his big sister, Gold. "We barely got any rest."

"But that's OK. Who knows when B.O.R.T.R.O.N. will have another assignment for us? Remember after Paris? We had to wait nine months before going on the Cuba mission," argued Eddie.

"Yeah, Eddie is right, Gold," said Kian. "We're lucky to go again so soon, and B.O.R.T.R.O.N. said back-to-back missions have never happened before, so this is cool! If we finish early, maybe I can try out some of my magic tricks on the Italians."

The other kids crunched their faces in denial. Kian's tricks were terrible. Hopefully he wouldn't have a chance to do them in Italy.

"Hey Nikko," waved Eddie as he saw their friend waiting in front of Mr. Smith's house.

"Hi guys! Are you ready?" Nikko was excited to learn what the next mission was and whether there would be an opportunity for him to use his science, math, or technology skills to accomplish it. Nikko was the brains of the group, and the kids could count on him to solve problems that involved high-level thinking skills. It paid off for CLUB US to have a member with an engineer and an architect for parents.

"I'm hungry," said Eddie, mounting Mr. Smith's stairs.

"That's great," said Mr. Smith as he opened the screen door with a smile. "I thought you might be rushing and not have time for breakfast, so there's donuts and orange juice waiting for you."

CLUB US

"Cool!" said Kian as they walked into Mr. Smith's dining room.

They grabbed their favorite donuts and a glass of orange juice and sat down to wait for B.O.R.T.R.O.N.. It was almost eight.

"I wonder what our mission is going to be this time," said Eddie.

"Me too," said Cassie.

"Don't worry," said Mr. Smith. "As on the past missions, B.O.R.T.R.O.N. will explain everything you'll need to know."

"Hey, I hear a buzz," said Eddie.

"And a hum," said Kian.

"And another buzz!!!" exclaimed Nikko as they ran into the library in response to B.O.R.T.R.O.N.'s signal.

As soon as they entered, they saw the transporter's flashing lights, the signal that it was time to go.

 # CHAPTER 2
(Due)
~ doo-eh ~

"Good morning, everyone. Are you ready?" said the robot-like voice they had come to know and love.

"Yes!" said Eddie before anyone else could answer.

James Smith was proud of Eddie. He'd had so much faith in the kid that he'd introduced him to B.O.R.T.R.O.N.. Eddie had longed to be a member of CLUB US, but the others told him he was too young. Mr. Smith thought B.O.R.T.R.O.N. was just what the boy needed to gain entrance—and he was right. Though Eddie was in fourth grade and the others were all sixth graders, Mr. Smith knew he was up for any mission sent the team's way, and Eddie hadn't disappointed him.

B.O.R.T.R.O.N. had been in James Smith's family for generations. His grandfather was the first to experience exciting adventures in the Accelerated Speed and Distance (ASD) Transporter. According to tradition, brave, intelligent, and confident children, aged ten to eighteen, were chosen to travel with the transporter to solve global dilemmas. Youth were selected for these missions because adults had done such a bad job at creating global harmony. At age eighteen, when team captains reached adulthood, B.O.R.T.R.O.N. went to another ten-year-old somewhere in the world.

The transporter had returned to Mr. Smith when his son turned ten. He was thrilled that Jimmy would have the opportunity to participate in the important missions, just as he had as a boy. Sadly, Jimmy was killed in a car accident at age fourteen, along with James's wife, Elizabeth. Mr. Smith's life was changed forever. His family meant the world to him and losing them was almost too much to bear.

When the transporter returned to him the previous year and asked if he thought Eddie and his friends would be good crew candidates, there was no doubt in his mind that they would do an excellent job. And it excited him to know his young friends would experience what he and his son had.

"OK, guys, here's the assignment," began B.O.R.T.R.O.N., as the kids gathered on the floor in front of Mr. Smith's desk. "As I told you yesterday, this challenge will take you to Italy, the birthplace of Gold and Eddie. Even though they were quite young when they left, they might remember something that will be helpful to you.

"This assignment is unique in many ways. First of all, there's never been a back-to-back mission, and I'm just as shocked as you are that it's happening. You just got home from Cuba yesterday, and we all learned together that another mission was pending. Now I have all the details," continued the transporter.

"Galotta Automobiles, an Italian firm, is the largest transportation manufacturer in Italy. In addition to automobiles, trucks, buses, ambulances, and other street vehicles, it produces railway cars and engines, military vehicles, farm tractors, and more. The firm has enjoyed huge success for generations, and now it is in jeopardy.

"For the past five years its biggest competitor, Berti Motors, has infiltrated Galotta's data centers with masterminds who have hacked the computer systems of all its vehicles. They have implemented a well-thought-out plan that will cause every Galotta engine in Italy to melt down on the same day, at the same time. If the plan is successful, not only will vehicles througout the country be destroyed, but millions of lives will also be lost. Berti Motors has only one goal: to replace all the ruined Galottas with its own products. It will sell them at cost, to those who are victims of the meltdown, and Berti Motors will become Italy's leader in transportation manufacturing."

The room was silent. No one, not even Eddie, said a word.

"I told you this mission was unique because it came back-to-back to a previous assignment; however, there's more," said B.O.R.T.R.O.N..

Cassie put her head down and placed her hand on her forehead to cover her eyes. *This can't be happening. . . again,* she thought. *I promised myself to get out of this club last time and here I am again.*

Gold knew what Cassie was thinking and realized she might have to do some negotiating to keep her from abandoning the mission.

"When you get to Italy, you will have two important tasks," said B.O.R.T.R.O.N..

"Two?!" said Kian and Nikko simultaneously.

"Epic!" said Eddie.

"Yes, two. You must first meet with Giancarlo Galotta, the CEO of Galotta Automobiles, in Rome, to warn him of the plot. Then you must go to Capri to find Otello Berti, and explain the unimaginable damage that will be done if the deadly plan goes through.

"This is a big mission. You will have to travel to different parts of Italy and do it fast. There will be no time to spare.

"As always, you will have twenty-four hours to complete your mission, which is twenty-four minutes here in Hamilton City. You must meet me back at Trevi Fountain on time, or I will leave without you. Are you still up for the challenge?"

B.O.R.T.R.O.N. saw four of the kids in

obvious agreement. Cassie still sat with her head down and her hand on her forehead.

Gold touched Cassie's shoulder, and the girl lifted her eyes to look at her friend. Gold didn't have to say anything; Cassie knew what she was thinking and couldn't let her down. Ever since her mom had passed, Gold was there for her more than anyone in her life. She owed her so much. Cassie wanted to back out, but instead she took a deep breath, looked at the rest of the crew—and at B.O.R.T.R.O.N.—and slowly nodded her head.

CHAPTER 3
(Tre)
~ treh ~

"OK, you guys know the drill," everyone heard B.O.R.T.R.O.N. say.

The team knew what had to be done, and they were ready. Eddie walked over to give Mr. Smith a hug.

The kids were excited about what was in store. It was their third mission and they knew that more thrills and adventure awaited them. Even more importantly, they were aware that a successful mission would save lives and property. They had

Intrigue in Italy

to stay focused and remember that the completion of their assignment was their only goal.

Eddie was just as eager as the others, but he didn't look forward to saying goodbye to his best friend, Barks. His Kooikerhondje dog looked sad, but he was getting used to it. As hard as it was to be separated from his friend, Barks knew Eddie would be back faster than when he went to school every day. Even though they would only be gone for twenty-four minutes, the crew would have twenty-four hours in Italy to accomplish the mission. Flying through a rotating black hole, brought them into an altered time zone, which made it possible.

Barks was sitting at Mr. Smith's feet. Eddie gave him a hug and said, "Hey bud, I'll be back before you know it. And this time I'm going to bring you a souvenir, I promise!" Eddie saw his pet's tail wag, and it made him feel better. Barks gave him one of his sloppiest kisses, and even though it drenched him with drool, it was just what he needed. And now that Eddie had made his buddy the promise, he was going to have to find a dog souvenir in Italy. He wondered if that was possible.

The crew members stood in a circle, nervous as always, but also confident that they would complete their assignment. This mission was going to be especially dangerous because they had to accomplish not one, but two tasks. They were all up for the challenge. They stretched their arms into the center of the circle and touched index fingers. Right away they felt themselves shrinking down to the two-inch size required to travel in the transporter.

"Bye Mr. Smith," said Kian. "We'll be back before you know it."

They all waved and walked up the ramp.

Slowly, the door closed as Barks stood up and watched his friends disappear. Once inside the cabin, the kids sat down, felt their seat belts automatically buckle around them, and prepared themselves for B.O.R.T.R.O.N.'s ascent. As soon as they reached flying altitude, the screen lit up and the digital face appeared. Even though they knew it was still B.O.R.T.R.O.N. talking to them, hearing instructions from the screen made everything feel more thrilling.

"Italy is about as far away as France, so it's not going to take us too long to get there," said B.O.R.T.R.O.N..

"Wow, Paris was fun; maybe we could stop by and visit with our friends Sylvie and Guy," interrrupted Eddie.

"No friend visits, Eddie. This mission is going to take every minute of your time, so you must use it carefully. You need to focus on getting the job done and returning to me on time, or you may regret it," warned B.O.R.T.R.O.N..

Eddie realized his comment was a mistake.

More than anything, he wanted the other kids, and B.O.R.T.R.O.N., to realize he was a serious member of the team and could be counted on.

"So, give us more details, B.O.R.T.R.O.N.," said Gold. "We're ready to do the job and do it quickly."

"Right," said Nikko. "We're listening."

"You already know the plan by Berti Motors to destroy Galotta vehicles all over the country. Now let me tell you exactly what you need to do to stop them.

"We will land on the rooftop of a hotel right across the street from Trevi Fountain. The fountain is one of the most famous monuments in the world, and one that is visited by millions of tourists every year. The hotel is called Relais Hotel de la Fontana Trevi; remember that, just in case you need it."

Gold typed the hotel name into her cell phone.

"You will have a chance to grow back to

normal size on the roof because no one will be there. Then, take the back stairs down to the first floor, so you aren't spotted going through the hotel.

"As soon as you walk out the front door, you will see Trevi Fountain. There's a tradition in Rome that if a visitor to the fountain throws in a coin, he or she will have good luck. Even though our time is tight, it will just take a few seconds to do it, and having good luck never hurts on our missions. It's important, however, that you hold the coin with your right hand and throw it over your left shoulder. That's the only way it will work."

"It also means you will come back to Rome one day," said Nikko. "My parents once had a big job to work with an Italian architectural company here in Rome, and they told me all about it."

"You're right, Nikko," chuckled the transporter.

"From the fountain, walk down the street to your right to find a restaurant called Trattoria

Scavolino Roma. This is where Giancarlo Galotta has coffee every morning. Hopefully the restaurant won't be too full and you'll be able to talk to him privately. You'll recognize him because he has a headful of gray hair, a gray mustache and beard, and smokes a big cigar. He laughs a lot and will be with friends.

"You must warn him of the plan Berti Motors has in place so that he can do whatever he can on his end to stop the plan. He, of course, has access to the master computer center, and hopefully he can step in and help.

"After that, go to the island of Capri in the southern part of Italy. You'll have to take a train to Naples, a bus to the Amalfi Coast, and afterward a hydrofoil ferry to Capri. Once there, you will go to Otello Berti's villa at the top of the hill and convince him to stop the meltdown.

"This is the most important part of the mission. Show him the video that clearly, and scientifically, explains that not only vehicles but millions of lives will be lost if he goes through with his plan. There are no other options. Otello Berti is not a bad man, but he is planning a very bad deed. Do you understand exactly what is needed from you?"

It was a lot. The kids looked a little unsure, then Eddie spoke up and said, "Relais Hotel de la Fontana Trevi, check. Take the back steps down, check. Throw a coin over our left shoulders into the fountain, check. Go to the Trattoria Scavolino Roma restaurant on the street to the right of the fountain and find Giancarlo Galotta to explain what's going on, check. We'll easily recognize him because he has gray hair, gray mustache, gray beard, smokes a cigar, and hangs out with his buddies, check."

"Well done, Eddie," said B.O.R.T.R.O.N.. "Does anyone remember what happens next?"

Before any of the crew could answer, Eddie

continued. "Take the train to Naples, check. Grab a bus to Amalfi Coast, check. Take the hydrofoil ferry over to the island of Capri, check. Go to Otello's villa at the top of the hill, check. Explain to him the extent of the damage that will occur from the meltdown and get him to stop it, check. Meet you and head home." *Whew!* thought Eddie, hoping he had remembered everything.

The kids all gave him a round of applause and a high five, and he felt like a hero. *Now we just have to do it!* he thought.

"It sounds like you've got it," said B.O.R.T.R.O.N.. "Any questions?"

Cassie opened her mouth and the other kids shot her a dirty look. Cassie doubted everything, and this time they didn't want to hear any pushback. They had a big mission. They were excited, and they knew they could get it done if everyone worked together.

"Cassie, it looks like you were going to

say something. Do you have a question?" asked B.O.R.T.R.O.N..

"Oh no," responded Cassie, feeling the eyes of the others on her. She forced a smile and continued, "I was just going to say, 'Awesome!'"

Her friends were relieved and hoped that once she got there, she'd be just as excited as they were.

"As always, you will have translators, euros, and candies representing almost any kind of food you might want to eat. Most important is the USB flash drive with the video that explains not only the mechanical and technological reasons the mission must be stopped, but also the moral and human reasons why. I am hoping that if one line of convincing doesn't work, the other one will. It's going to be up to you to use them both if necessary," said the transporter.

"I am entrusting the information to you, Gold. You can show it to Giancarlo Galotta and

CLUB US

Otello Berti on your cell or have them scan the QR code on the outside of the drive and it will download to their phones.

"We are currently hovering over the fountain. I'm going to land now if everyone's questions have been answered. Remember, you must meet me here by 8:27 tomorrow morning, or I will return without you."

They felt the descent of the transporter and gathered everything they needed to disembark. Gold retrieved the USB drive from the slot in B.O.R.T.R.O.N.'s dashboard and scanned the QR code to copy it to her phone for safekeeping. She wasn't sure what to expect, but wanted to have all her bases covered. She then safely tucked the drive into her jacket and zipped the pocket closed.

"Good job, Gold," said B.O.R.T.R.O.N.. "I saw the extra precautions you took to safeguard the information on the USB drive, and if I had a thumb, I would give you a thumbs-up."

They all laughed and everyone was sure that Gold would do a great job. According to her and Cassie, girls ruled. Now the rest of the crew would see if they were right.

The door slowly opened, and they stepped out. They waved goodbye to B.O.R.T.R.O.N. and scurried behind an air-conditioning unit to grow back to normal size. The door closed, B.O.R.T.R.O.N. started to ascend, and on the way blinked the lights to say "good luck."

It was showtime!

CHAPTER 4
(Quattro)
~ kwaht-troh ~

The crew quickly found the back steps and headed down to the lobby. When they opened the door to exit the building, instead of seeing a reception area, they found themselves on a floor with doors that looked like guest rooms.

"Hey, what's going on?" said Kian. "The sign on the door said 'one,' but this doesn't look like a hotel lobby to me."

"It must be like in France," said Gold, "where the first floor is above the lobby. Let's go down one more." They reentered the back-stair area and went down one more floor. This door said PORTINERIA, and to be sure, Cassie repeated it into the translator. They all heard "lobby."

When they walked out, the very first person they saw was a security guard. "Buongiorno," he said with a smile.

"Buongiorno," answered Gold, correctly assuming it meant "good morning."

They walked across a small room with floor-to-ceiling windows and out the front door. As B.O.R.T.R.O.N. promised, right in front of them was the Trevi Fountain. It was so magnificent, they all stood there with their mouths hanging open.

Though the buildings on the streets to the right and left of the monument looked like ordinary offices or apartments, the fountain, statues, and structure in front of them looked as if they had been built hundreds of years ago. Every aspect of the display was gleaming white, and in the center was an impressive statue of a Roman god. He was muscular with curly hair and a long beard, and wore a flowing cape that wrapped around his body. On each side of him stood a female statue, one with a bowl of fruit and the other holding a snake. In front were two huge seahorses rising from enormous boulders that jutted out from the fountain's waters and two warriors who were controlling them. The entire scene emerged out of a block-long, majestic fountain with cascading blue water.

They wanted to stand there and admire, but Gold reminded them: "We don't have a lot of time. Let's throw our coins into the fountain and find Giancarlo."

It was only a quarter to nine, but the area was starting to get crowded. They all took a coin from their translator drawers and walked over to the fountain. They turned their backs, held the coins in their right hands, and threw them over their left shoulders. . . all except Cassie. She was so amazed by the monument, she forgot which shoulder to throw it over and threw it over the right one.

"Cassie!" said Kian. "You threw the coin over the wrong shoulder. You're going to bring us bad luck."

"Oh no," she cried. She turned and saw her coin at the bottom of the fountain. She remembered exactly what it looked like and jumped in to get it. Within seconds, she emerged from the water soaking wet, but had a smile on her face.

"I got it," she said excitedly, holding it up for everyone to see. At that moment, two uniformed men with *Polizia* written in big yellow letters on the back of their shirts, came their way in a hurry.

"Uh oh, looks like we're in trouble. We'd better get out of here," said Eddie.

"Cassie, throw the coin over your left shoulder! We gotta go," said Kian.

Cassie held the coin in her right hand and quickly threw it over her left shoulder, then took off running behind the rest of the crew.

"Fermatavi!" yelled one of officers.

They didn't need a translator for that one. They were so used to being chased by the police on their other missions, they knew it meant stop. The language was different, but the urgency in the officer's voice was the same.

They ran down the street to the right of the monument, the police at their heels. At the first corner, they saw a group of nuns in the garden of a convent. They dashed into the garden and hid behind a row of bushes. The nuns didn't notice them, so they kept low and watched the policemen run right past them.

"Whew," said Eddie, standing up with the others. "That was close."

"Buongiorno bambini, cosa ci fate qui?" asked one of the nuns, walking over to them with a smile.

"No Italiano," said Eddie, touching his

mouth and shaking his head. He put the translator near her face and pointed to it, hoping she would repeat what she'd previously said. She was startled by the machine and took a step back, still smiling, then caught on to what he wanted her to do.

Though still a bit confused, she repeated, "Buongiorno bambini, cosa ci fate qui?"

"Good morning children, what are you doing here?" translated the machine.

The nun laughed out loud when she heard the translation, then Eddie said, "We are playing a game with our schoolmates."

"Stiamo giocando con i nostri compagni di scuola," repeated the translator.

"Bene, molto bene," she said.

Even though they weren't sure what she had said, it sounded good, and she was still smiling, so they thought it was time for them to slip away.

"Ciao, sorella," said Nikko. He had repeated "Bye, sister," into the translator while Eddie was explaining why they were there.

It worked.

"Ciao, ragazzi," said the nun.

"*Ragazzi* must mean kids," said Cassie and repeated it into the translator. "Yep, that's exactly what it means, good to know."

They continued down the street, searching for the restaurant where Giancarlo Galotta had his daily breakfast. They stopped to take a look at the city map near the bus stop and saw Trattoria Scavolino Roma. It wasn't very far, so they started walking the few blocks to get there.

Within minutes, they entered Giancarlo's morning meeting place. In the front of the restaurant was a mouthwatering display of Italian pastries. Behind the counter were several chefs and waitresses chatting. They appeared to be friends or family, as the conversation was lively.

The kids heard a roaring laugh coming from the back corner. When they turned in that direction,

Intrigue in Italy

there he was, gray hair, gray beard, a big cigar, and a contagious smile. He was sitting with some people who were speaking English, and the kids wondered if they were American.

As they approached the table, Kian said, "Excuse me, are you Mr. Galotta?"

The gray-haired man turned to the kids. "Well, yes I am. What can I do for you, ragazzi?" he said, smiling from ear to ear and puffing on his cigar.

"We have something very important to tell you. Do you think we could speak to you alone?" asked Gold.

Giancarlo let out a big laugh. *Who are these American kids?* he asked himself. "Of course, you can; let's go over there," he responded, standing up and looking back at his friends with amusement.

They all walked over to a bigger table and sat down with the larger-than-life Italian.

Gold explained, "Signor Galotta, we are

here because there is a threat to destroy millions of Galotta vehicles around the country. Not only will drivers and pedestrians be in danger, but also people in ambulances, trains, buses, and other vehicles produced by your company."

Giancarlo put down his cigar, leaned forward, and stared silently at the children.

"What are you talking about? Is this a joke?" he finally asked without a smile.

"It's not a joke, Signor Galotta," said Nikko. "It's a very real threat, and we've been sent here to let you know so you can do what you can to try to stop it. I know we're kids, but please believe us. If your competitor's plan is not stopped, there will be millions of lives lost, and Galotta Automiles will be destroyed."

My competitor? Giancarlo thought. *Could they possibly be talking about Otello Berti?*

"Berti Motors has hacked the computer systems of all vehicles manufactured by Galotta

Automobiles," continued Nikko.

So, they were *talking about Otello!* Even though they had parted ways many, many years ago, Giancarlo thought they still shared a mutual respect for one another. He didn't believe what he was hearing. Was someone playing a trick on him?

"Hackers began infiltrating your data center five years ago, and have programmed the computers in every single Galotta vehicle in the country to simultaneously melt down tomorrow morning at seven o'clock. All the details of what they have done are explained in a video on this USB drive," said Gold, handing Giancarlo the drive from her pocket. "Or you can view it on my cell phone."

He grabbed her phone and clicked on the video. His face turned white. He was obviously shaken and angry. When the video finished, he threw the cell phone on the table and said, "I don't believe you," then got up and walked back to where his friends were waiting.

"What's going on, Giancarlo?" asked the English-speaking woman.

"These kids are telling me that Berti Motors has a plan to destroy Galotta Automobiles and kill millions of people in the process," he said in a whisper.

The gasps from everyone at the table were so loud that every customer in the restaurant turned and looked their way.

"I don't believe them, but what if it is true?" he continued. "We need to figure out if these ragazzi know what they are talking about, and if they do, we must stop Otello's plan immediately!"

He stood from the table, turned to one of the men sitting with him and said, "Bring those kids to my office," then hastily left the restaurant.

"Let's get out of here," said Eddie. "It looks like that guy is coming after us." Not sure if they were in trouble or not, they didn't want to take any chances. They headed toward the door, and so did the man. Once outside, the kids ran as fast as they could back to the convent. It was the only place they knew, and they thought they'd be able to hide out there again. The man ran after them. Gold took a right, and the kids followed. When they reached the convent, they ran into the garden and once again hid in the same place. They waited a few minutes, peeked through the bushes, but didn't see Giancarlo's man.

"State ancora giocando con i vostri amici?" asked the same nun they'd met earlier, as she approached the bushes. The kids were afraid to stand, so Nikko handed her his translator from his crouching position, and she repeated the question into it.

"Still playing with your friends?" said the translator.

"Si sorella, si," whispered Nikko with a hesitant smile, while peeping through the bushes to see if the man was coming.

Just as they started inching their way out of the garden, Giancarlo's man entered and loomed above them.

"Come with me. Signor Galotta wants to talk to you again," he said.

At that moment, the nun stepped in between the man and the kids. "Non può portare questi bambini," she said, pointing her index finger at him.

She told him he couldn't take the children, and he knew he couldn't force her to do it. It would cause an embarrassment to his boss, for which he would surely get fired. He bowed his head and said "Si sorella," as he backed out of the garden.

Once he returned to the sidewalk, he took out his cell phone to call Giancarlo and let him know what had happened. There was no answer, so he headed back to the office to face the music.

"Grazie, sorella," said Nikko.

She pointed to his translator and when he

took it out, she spoke into it still with a smile, "Ora andate a trovare i vostri amici." The translator said, "Now go find your friends."

They all laughed and waved goodbye to the nun. She walked toward the door of the convent, shaking her head and muttering "ragazzi" with a smile.

CHAPTER 5
(Cinque)
~ cheen-kweh ~

They weren't exactly sure where they were, but they knew they had to get to the Tiburtina train station as fast as possible. As they checked the city map on the corner, a woman approached them.

"Can I help you find something?" she asked in English.

"Yes, we're trying to get to the Tiburtina train station," said Kian.

"Oh, it's very close," she responded, turning to point it out on the map.

Gold stood back and looked at the lady closely. There was something about her that seemed familiar. Then she noticed her long red and black earrings, and realized she had been sitting at Giancarlo's table in the restaurant. They needed to get away from her as quickly as possible.

Gold quietly touched each of her friends on their back shoulder and gave them the signal to get out of there. They backed away quietly, and when the woman turned around, they were already halfway down the street.

She quickly punched a number into her cell phone and said, "They're heading down Via della Mercede. Hurry and you will catch them!"

The kids raced through a pedestrian plaza in the hopes of escaping whoever was chasing them, when they heard the woman shout, "There they are!"

People were moving out of the way, wondering what was going on. The crew saw a narrow passageway and ran down it. Suddenly, the back door of one of the businesses opened, and a girl beckoned for them to come in. They followed her, certain that otherwise they were going to be caught. Once inside, they saw they were in the back of a restaurant.

"I saw you running through the plaza and thought you might be in trouble," said the girl. "When you turned the corner, I went out back to see if I could find you. What's going on? Why are they chasing you?"

"We're not sure why they're chasing us, but we don't want to get into trouble," said Gold. "We need help."

The girl wasn't sure what was happening, but she knew it wasn't right for adults to be chasing children.

"Stay here. I'm going to check the plaza to see if they're still there." She went through the restaurant, out to the plaza and the kids waited.

"What if they're out there? What will we do?" asked Cassie.

The girl rushed back into the small room. "They're looking for you everywhere," she said. "Let me check out back to see if it might be safe for you to leave that way." She opened the back door, and saw the man and woman standing at the entrance to the passageway. She recognized them as the same people who had been chasing the kids.

"You can't go out that way either. Let me think," said the girl.

"Maybe you could tell them we're in here, and we can slip out before they get down the passageway," said Gold.

"Good idea. I'll check, and if they're not looking, I'll give you a signal. Sneak out and hide behind the dumpster to the right. Then I'll tell them you're inside the restaurant."

The girl partially opened the door and whispered to the kids, "Come on."

CLUB US

One by one, they slipped outside and hid behind the dumpster.

"They're here!" yelled the girl, walking towards the man and woman, while pointing to the open door of the restaurant.

As planned, they raced down the passageway, and into the door. When they did, the kids took off toward the other end. They paused at the exit, and waved a thank-you to the girl. She smiled, returned the wave and closed the door behind her.

Intrigue in Italy

CHAPTER 6
(Sei)
~ seh-ee ~

Now the CLUB US crew really had to hurry. They remembered from the map that the Colosseum was nearby. This was good news because the Tiburtina station, where they would take the train to Naples, was just on the other side. According to the map, however, the only way to get there was to walk around the Colosseum which would take time.

"Maybe we can cut through the monument and get to the station faster," said Kian.

"I don't know. . ." said Gold. "Let's ask

someone." She spoke into the translator: "Is it possible to go through the Colosseum to get to the Tiburtina train station?" The machine gave her the translation but rather than try to remember it, she said *buongiorno* to a friendly looking lady, and when the lady smiled, she pushed the button. The translator said it again in Italian.

The lady was startled and started to laugh; then she said, "Si, si," and waved for them to follow her. She walked with them to the Colosseum entrance. Once there, she pointed forward to let them know that if they walked straight across, they would get to the station.

"Grazie," said Gold.

"Prego," said the lady as she walked off smiling.

They entered the Colosseum and were stunned. It was so much larger than they expected, and they could barely see the exit on the other end. There was no roof, and the sun beat down on them.

The center was a maze of tunnels under what used to be the main arena floor, and they guessed that was where the animals were kept until time for them to fight the gladiators. Most of the structure had been destroyed, but it was easy to imagine where thousands of people sat on rock bleachers, to observe the entertainment.

"This is epic," said Eddie. "It's hard to imagine gladiator and animal fights taking place thousands of years ago right where we're standing."

"Yeah," said Nikko. "And in some fights, the gladiators were beheaded."

"*Eeew*," said the other kids. "That's gross, Nikko."

"Well, it's true," he responded with a laugh.

"We're in trouble," said Cassie, pointing to a sign blocking the stairs to enter the passageways and pass through the Colosseum.

The sign read CHIUSO, in Italian and about fifteen other languages. If it was closed, they had no choice but to walk around the entire monument, and who knew how long that would take.

They exited the building and started walking to their left. There were so many tourists they could barely move. They began to worry that they were going to miss their train.

Suddenly, Eddie said, "Hey guys, check this out."

There was a stand with Segway scooters to rent—ten euros for thirty minutes. Hopefully they wouldn't need them that long, so they each put ten euros into a slot with an available Segway and took off. They held on tightly to the waist-high handlebars to access the hand brakes if needed. The sidewalks were crowded with people, but there was a special lane for Segways, and they zipped along. It was a lot of fun and gave them a chance to relax, even though they had to pay careful attention to the pedestrians to avoid an accident.

As they traveled, they were still able to view

the sites, especially the majestic exterior of the Colosseum. Even though gladiator and animal fights were no longer held there—and certainly not beheadings—the mystique of the structure was the same as it was on grand opening day two thousand years ago.

"That was fun," said Kian as they returned the Segways on the other side of the building.

"And I'm all dry!" said Cassie.

# CHAPTER 7
(Sette)
~ set-teh ~

Inside the train station was a sea of madness—hundreds of people going in hundreds of directions with hundreds of announcements being made over the loudspeaker. There were huge electronic boards high up on every wall, with fast-changing yellow digital names of the places the trains were going and the times they were headed there. The kids looked at the boards and finally Nikko said, "There's a train to Naples leaving in fifteen minutes on Track 8."

Intrigue in Italy

They hurried to the window to buy tickets, then wasted no time looking for the track. There were so many trains ready to take off in different directions around Italy, that they had to maneuver their way through the throngs of people waiting to board.

"Here's Track 8," said Gold.

The kids jumped on the first car they saw, but Nikko stopped them, saying, "I think this says First Class. Prima Classe—it's almost the same in Spanish."

They walked down the platform to find the right car. The last thing they wanted was more police chasing them. Finally, they found a car whose sign read SECONDA CLASSE. They glanced at their tickets, and confirmed that was where they needed to be. They jumped onboard, and before they got to their seats, they felt the train heading out of the station.

Cassie and Gold relaxed in window seats

across from each other, and the three boys grabbed spots on the other side of the aisle. The view got prettier and prettier as they rode, but they were so tired from the hectic morning that they soon fell asleep.

~ ~ ~

They felt themselves being shaken awake and heard female voices talking to them. When they opened their eyes and looked up, they saw two ladies dressed in dark blue uniforms with matching caps.

Oh no, what did we do now? Cassie asked herself.

"Biglietti?" asked one of the inspectors. The kids were confused.

Nikko said "biglietti" into the translator and told the kids the ladies were asking for their tickets. They pulled them out and showed them to the inspectors.

"Do you speak English?" asked one of them.

"Yes," said Gold.

"These tickets are not for today. They are for tomorrow."

"What!?" said Cassie. "Oh my gosh."

"If you have a credit card, I can sell you a new ticket," continued the woman.

"We don't have a credit card," said Gold. "But we can pay you in cash."

"Sorry, my terminal only accepts cards. You will have to get off at the next stop and make an exchange."

"This is crazy! We don't speak Italian, and we made a mistake," pleaded Cassie. "We'll never have time to exchange the tickets and get back on the train before it takes off again."

"I'm sorry," the inspector responded.

The kids were speechless. Now what? They looked at the map posted on the wall. The next stop was Cassino.

"There's nothing we can do. Let's just get off

and try to figure it out," said Gold calmly.

"If you say so," said Cassie, plopping back down in her seat.

When they arrived at Cassino, the inspectors were standing at the end of the car. Even if the kids had thought about staying on the train, there was no way they were going to be able to do it.

They walked to the exit, descended three steps to the platform, and found themselves in a train station quite unlike the one in Rome. There were no other trains on either of the two tracks; no people waiting to board; no announcements being made; and when they walked into the waiting room, it was empty.

"This must really be a small town," said Nikko.

"If the station is any indication, I'd say you're right," said Cassie.

"Let's check it out," said Kian, walking through the front door. The street outside was quiet with a few taxis, their drivers napping as they waited. Most of the passengers were being greeted by friends and family members, and when their cars departed, the crew members found themselves alone.

They went back into the station to ask for directions. The shade had been pulled down on the window of the ticket office, and there was no one around who might be able to help. They saw a map on the wall that said they were only twenty-five minutes from Naples, but the next train wasn't arriving in Cassino for four hours.

"Maybe we could get there by taxi. Let's find out," said Nikko.

They went outside and saw a minivan taxi waiting in line. Gold walked over to the driver and said, "Amalfi Coast?"

The young driver promptly put his cap on his headfull of blond hair and answered, "Si, signorina! Duecento venticinque euro."

"Duecento venticinque?" Gold repeated, calculating if they could swing it,

She barely got the words out before Nikko answered, "Two hundred and twenty-five euros? That's crazy!"

"Is there a cheaper way?" Nikko said into the translator.

"Si!" said the driver after hearing the translation. "Taxi to Pompeii settanta cinque," flashing the fingers on both hands seven times, then the fingers on one hand one more time.

"Seventy-five!" said Eddie. "That's not bad."

"And after," continued the driver, slowly in English. "Dieci euros in bus to Sorrento," putting up just one set of ten fingers.

"Perfect," said Nikko, jumping into the passenger seat while the rest of the crew took seats in the middle and back.

"Allora, andiamo!" said the driver as he sped away with a smile.

"Yep! Let's go!" said Nikko.

They continued south on a road that ran close to the train tracks and saw more of the beautiful scenery they had experienced when riding the train from Rome. They passed a church, a cemetery, spacious parks, and museums. If they weren't in such a hurry, they would have liked to explore the countryside, but they had to get to Capri as quickly as possible. Taking the taxi was a great decision because now they would be able to go right past Naples without stopping. That should allow them to make up the time they lost getting kicked off the train.

When they reached Pompeii, each of the kids paid the driver fifteen euros and waved goodbye.

They walked to the terminal where six buses were parked and looked at the sign listing all the departure times.

"The next bus to Amalfi Coast is leaving in two hours," said Gold.

CLUB US

"Hey, why don't we visit Pompeii while we wait?" asked Nikko. "That should be fun."

"Can we do it and still get back here on time to catch the bus?" asked Cassie.

"Sure, we have plenty of time," said Nikko.

"Awesome!" said Kian.

"We'd better not miss that bus. . ." said Cassie.

CHAPTER 8
(Otto)
~ oht-toh ~

They got in line and bought five general admission tickets. As soon as they entered the grounds of Pompeii, they knew they were someplace special. They walked the old cobblestone streets, went inside the remains of one-story buildings that were built thousands of years ago, and saw fragments of what had once been magnificent Roman statues.

"Pompeii is a cool place," said Kian. We studied it in history class."

On display in glass boxes, they saw the bodies

of people and animals that had been petrified by ash and lava from the volcano eruption. It looked as though the lava caught some of them while they were running.

They walked over to a group with an English-speaking tour guide and heard her explain, "On August 24, 79 AD, at around one o'clock in the afternoon, Mount Vesuvius, which you can still see there, erupted." She pointed to the mountain behind them. "The city trembled and buildings began to crumble. By five o'clock everything was covered by ash, and buildings caught on fire. Lava spewed from the volcano and covered the entire city and many of the people. Twenty-four hours later, Pompeii was completely buried and over two thousand people were dead. Within a few years, no one could remember where the city had once stood."

"It's hard to believe what we're seeing, but it really happened," said Nikko. "When was the city rediscovered? Wasn't it around 1700 or 1800?" he asked the guide.

"Very good young man," she replied. "You are correct. Pompeii remained mostly untouched until 1748, when a group of explorers arrived in Campania and began to dig. They found that the ashes had acted as a marvelous preservative and underneath all that dust, the city was almost exactly as it had been nearly two thousand years before."

"Nikko, you're amazing," said Cassie.

Her comment made him feel good. His parents had always taught him that his intelligence was something people would appreciate one day.

Eddie looked at the time on his phone. "This is super interesting, but we'd better get back to the bus stop. It's going to leave in about twenty minutes," he said. Even though the kids wanted to stay and learn more, it was time to return to the entrance of the long-lost city.

"It's too bad we can't tell anyone about what

we're seeing. It's going to be hard to keep quiet about this place," said Kian.

Within a few minutes they were back at the entrance. The bus to the Amalfi Coast was waiting and they crossed the street and boarded.

"Buongiorno!" said the driver with a smile as she collected ten euros from each of them in return for a ticket. Within minutes they were on their way.

The bus wove around narrow roads and through tiny towns. The kids enjoyed the beautiful countryside full of farm animals, wineries, restaurants, and homes as well as people riding bicycles and driving Galottas everywhere.

"This is so different than everything we know," said Cassie. "And it's awesome."

"We're right about at the ankle," said Nikko.

"The ankle? What are you talking about?" asked Kian.

"You know. . . the country of Italy looks like

a high-heeled boot, and we're right about at the ankle," he said.

"Ha! You're right, Nikko; we'll be on the Amalfi Coast soon, way before getting to the toe," said Cassie.

They all laughed at the comparisons and felt excited that they were almost at their destination.

About half an hour later, they reached Sorrento. It was one of the first cities on the Amalfi Coast, and from there they would take the hydrofoil ferry over to Capri. They got off the bus and hurried over to the port.

The marina was full of boats of all sizes, colors, and shapes.

"How will we know which one to take?" asked Kian.

"Why don't we ask at the ticket counter?" said Gold.

There were several places to buy tickets, so they walked to the one with the shortest line. When they reached the window, Gold said, "Capri," and held up five fingers.

The man behind the counter smiled and said, "Cinquanta euro," and showed them the receipt with the total price.

"Fifty euros," said Kian.

"Ask him what time the next hydrofoil ferry is leaving," said Nikko.

Gold repeated the question into the translator, and held it up so the man could hear. "A che ora parte il prossimo aliscafo?"

The man smiled and pointed to the sign on the outside of the booth.

"OK, we have ten minutes, and the hydrofoil is right over there," said Cassie, pointing to a boat that looked like a sleek version of the ferry at Disneyworld.

They each gave the man ten euros and took their tickets.

"Grazie," said Gold.

Intrigue in Italy

They walked toward the departure gate, bought an ice cream from a lady with a small cart, then boarded. Inside the ferry were rows and rows of seats. It looked like a movie theater. Along both sides were huge windows with clear views of the ocean.

"Let's go up to the top deck," said Kian, walking toward a small staircase. The view at the top was even more spectacular.

When they took off, the movement of the waves in the crystal-clear blue water made it obvious they were traveling at a very high speed. The sun shone brightly over the ocean, and its rays created a glistening reflection on the surface. Sailors on small boats waved to them, and they waved back. They passed huge boats going a lot slower than their high-speed ferry, and they waved to those people as they sped past them too.

"Epic!" said Eddie.

"Look, we're almost there," said Cassie

as the shore of Capri came into view. "That was quick."

"Well, I guess it's not called high speed for nothing," laughed Gold.

From the ferry, the city was picturesque. Completely built into the side of a mountain, Capri looked like something from a travel brochure. Everything was quaint, clean, and colorful, and they were excited to explore.

They quickly disembarked. There were lots of people waiting for taxis. Drivers were standing next to their low, convertible cars, which had enough seating in the back to accommodate six passengers face-to-face and canvas covers to shield riders from the sun. They were pretty cool. The crew was in a hurry to meet with Otello Berti and went to the front of the line. No one said anything, probably because they were kids, so they took advantage.

A driver waiting by his taxi waved and said,

"Ciao ragazzi!"

"Ciao!" they all responded as they walked over to a yellow car that matched the driver's shirt and pants. He looked pretty fancy for a taxi driver, but they were in Capri, where the rich and famous lived and vacationed. Gold showed him the address of Otello Berti's villa.

"Do you know where this is?" she asked.

The driver looked at the paper and turned to her with a smile. "Villa Berti? Everyone knows the Berti family and exactly where their villa is. Hop in, ragazzi!"

"Are you American?" asked the driver in perfect English as he started winding up the hill.

"Yes, we are," responded Gold. "Your English is very good. Have you ever visited the U.S.?"

"Oh no, we study English in school because tourists are here all the time and many of them speak your language."

"Cool," said Kian. "It sure makes it a lot easier for us."

"So, why are you visiting the Bertis?" asked the driver.

"It's a long story," responded Gold.

The driver expertly climbed the hills, navigating the narrow roads that wrapped around the mountain on the way to the villa. The scene along the road was beautiful, full of lush bushes, flowering trees, and short brick walls or gates providing entrance into each of the immense homes that clearly belonged to wealthy owners. There were no commercial buildings on the road, no restaurants, no cafés, no shops—just extravagant landscaping and gates hiding private villas. The ride was peaceful and gave the kids a brief chance to relax.

"It's far," said Cassie.

"Actually, it is in Ana Capri, which is on a hill above Capri. The Bertis have a huge compound there with the main villa and several smaller houses for family members. Signor Berti is one of the richest men in Italy and has built a vacation home away from other villas for privacy," explained the driver.

"His vacation home?" said Nikko.

"Yes, he lives in Venice, but this is one of the homes he and his family visit often for vacation."

"Cool," said Kian.

At that moment, they rounded a corner and saw the huge Berti compound. As the driver said, there were a number of structures that encircled the property. As they drove to the entrance, they saw expanses of green landscaping, gorgeous flowers, sculpted bushes, and statues on the other side of a massive gate.

When they arrived at the front of the villa, they paid the driver and walked up to the guards.

"Do you want me to wait?" asked the driver.

"I don't think it will be necessary, but thank

you!" said Gold.

"Grazie," said the driver. "Ciao ragazzi!" he yelled as he jumped into his yellow convertible and headed back down the hill.

When the crew approached the gate, the guards eyed them without the slightest smile. The kids thought that was unusual for Italians, as almost everyone, so far, had been very friendly.

"Si?" said one of the guards.

They all knew that meant "yes," and from the tone of his voice, he wasn't in the mood for jokes, so Gold came right out and said, "Signor Berti per favore."

"Il Signor Berti non è qui e non tornerà per tre giorni," said the other guard.

The two men turned and walked away from the kids, and even though they didn't understand what he said, they knew the conversation was over.

"I don't want to ask him to repeat it into the translator, but we need to know what's going on," said Gold.

She ran behind the guards and once again said, "Signor Berti per favore." She then held the translator toward them.

A bit annoyed, the guard repeated, "Il Signor Berti non è qui e non tornerà per tre giorni. Arrivederci!"

"Mr. Berti is away and won't return for three days. Goodbye," said the translator.

"Three days!" said Cassie. "We have to see him before then."

The men had already reentered the guard house and closed the door. It was clear the kids needed to leave immediately.

"This is bad," said Nikko.

"Yes, it is because we don't have a Plan B, *and* we have no way of getting back to the city," said Cassie.

There was nothing, or no one, on the road. The air was so quiet, you could hear the chirping of the birds, and the splashes of people jumping into their private swimming pools.

"It doesn't look like we'll find a taxi here. Let's start walking. Going downhill is always easier than coming up," said Eddie.

The road was paved and easy to navigate by foot, especially since there wasn't any traffic. They guessed they would get back to Capri within an hour or so, as the route was a straight one. As they walked, however, they realized how dangerous it was going to be. The few cars that *were* on the road came perilously close to hitting them, since the sharp curves made it difficult to see pedestrians until one was right upon them.

"I don't know about this," said Eddie, jumping out of the way of an oncoming motorcycle.

Suddenly, they saw a small sign that read CAFÉ DE MOUNT SOLARO with an arrow pointing to the right.

"Let's go there and have something to drink

while we figure out our next move. There must be a better way for us to get down the mountain than on this crazy road," said Cassie.

"Maybe I can do some magic tricks for people in the café. I brought a deck of cards with me," said Kian.

No one said a word. They turned right, hoping the café would be empty, so Kian couldn't do his card tricks. They were the worst of all his bad illusions.

The small road ran much longer than they expected. It was a pleasant walk and at least they were safe from oncoming traffic because the road was narrow and cars couldn't drive there. Finally, they saw the café sitting on top of a remote hill. *Is this the only way to reach this café?* they wondered. If so, they felt confident there wouldn't be many people there.

Opening the latch of a small gate to gain entry from the quiet road, they were greeted with a breathtaking view of the Amalfi Coast. They could see for miles around on either side, including all the small towns, the clear blue water, and many small islands in this charming area of Italy. The patio café was completely empty so they had their choice of tables. As they sat down, the waiter came over with a smile and took their order.

While waiting for their fresh fruit juices, they noticed several empty lift seats that were positioned in both directions on a cable running to and from the café. It looked as though it went into town, but it was strange the lift chairs weren't moving.

When the waiter returned to the table with their drinks, he informed the crew that the lift was closed for repairs. This meant no one could access the mountaintop café from Capri, except by foot, as they had done.

"Oh boy," said Gold, twisting a curl by her right ear. This was going from bad to worse. They needed to come up with a way to get back down the mountain—and fast.

Eddie peered over the short brick wall by his chair. "Look guys," he said. "There's a staircase! We can take that down."

"Are you suggesting we walk down the side of this mountain? Did you see how tall it is?" asked Cassie.

"I did, but what's the alternative?"

"He's right," said Gold. "It's the only way, so let's get going."

They paid the bill and started the walk down. It wasn't as bad as they expected, and it seemed to be their only option.

After about fifty steps, the staircase stopped. Stopped. From that point, there was a narrow path filled with pebbles, rocks, and small creatures.

"Is this really happening?" said Cassie. "What are we going to do?"

"Here's what we're going to do, Cassie,"

said Gold. "We're going to continue walking until we get to the bottom. Let's be grateful this path is even here; otherwise, we'd have to maneuver down that road full of dangerous traffic, and we might not make it down safely. Ready, guys?"

"Ready," she heard, although no one sounded very enthusiastic.

"Then, let's go!"

They continued down the hill and as they went the route worsened. They passed other people coming up and were passed by some going down. Apparently, these were experienced hikers, as they had equipment like water, hiking shoes, and caps that protected their heads from the sun. The CLUB US crew had nothing—except the desperate desire to reach the bottom.

Soon they didn't see any more hikers, but they did see a little house in the middle of nowhere. Sitting alone on the tiny porch was a skinny, old lady who looked like the bad witch from a fairy tale. She was pretty frightening, so the kids said "Buongiorno" in friendly voices as they passed the house. She offered no response, just a cold stare.

"That's weird," said Kian. "We'd better keep our eyes and ears open for her. What if she comes after us?"

They looked around, but she still sat on the porch, legs crossed, smoking the big cigar. To be on the safe side, they looked back every few feet to make sure she was still there.

Finally, they reached a fork in the road. Without a compass or any idea where they were, no one knew which direction to take.

"What do you think?" Gold asked the group.

"I think we're in trouble," said Cassie.

Gold ignored her and said, "Let's go left."

Everyone followed. Their leader hoped she had made the right choice. A fork in the road was always a fifty-fifty decision; she crossed her fingers that she had bet on the right fifty.

CLUB US

At last, they began to see the town of Capri ahead of them. *Not too much farther to go*, everyone thought as they let out a collective sigh of relief knowing they would soon be back in civilization. In about twenty minutes, they reached another set of stairs that took them to a main road. The whole experience had been pretty scary, especially the skinny, old lady, but now they were back in familiar territory.

The crew tiptoed through a small cemetery at the bottom of the hill and soon found themselves in the center of town. Capri was filled with shops and restaurants and they plopped down at an outside table of a gelateria. The kids had always heard that the best gelato in the world was in Italy, and now they each needed a double scoop.

CHAPTER 9
(Nove)
~ noh-veh ~

The four-page gelato menu was filled with mouth-watering flavors, but they quickly realized they hadn't eaten all day and decided to go to the restaurant next door instead. They walked over to Gianni's Pizzeria and sat at a table covered with a red-and-white-checked tablecloth. Like at the gelateria, the pizza menu was to die for, and even though they had pizza-flavored candies in their translator drawers, they couldn't resist.

"This is Italy. We can't leave without having

some authentic pizza," said Kian with a laugh. Even though he didn't feel much like laughing, he knew somebody had to cheer the crowd up or the crew would never complete their mission.

Everyone chose his or her favorite pizza from the menu. As the waiter walked away, they heard a group of ladies talking in front of the nearby dress store. Nikko heard one of them say "Patricia" and something about Cuba. They were speaking Spanish, so he was paying extra-close attention.

Suddenly, he gasped and put his hands over his mouth.

"What, Nikko? What?" said Gold.

"That's Patricia Mendéz, the CEO of Mendéz Oil Company in Santiago. She's actually talking about us and our mission in Cuba."

"What?!" said Cassie.

"Remember? She was in Italy when we spoke to her by telephone yesterday. It makes sense that this could be where she was calling from," said

Nikko.

"Maybe she can help us," said Gold. "Besides, wouldn't it be great to meet her, if that really is Patricia Mendéz?"

Gold and Nikko walked over to the ladies while the others waited at the table.

"Señora Mendéz?" asked Nikko.

One of the women turned and looked at him with a puzzled expression. "Si," she responded slowly.

"Soy Nikko Martinez y ayer estuvimos en Santiago de Cuba para salvar la isla, ¿recuerda?" said Nikko, explaining in Spanish that they had been in her country yesterday to save the island.

"Dios mio!" said Patricia. "Oh my God! I am so happy to meet you. Thank you for everything; thank you *sooo* very much," she said, giving them both a big hug.

She told her friends that she would see them later, then walked over to the pizzeria with

Gold and Nikko to thank, and hug, the other crew members.

Patricia sat down at their table and asked, "What are you doing in Italy? And how in the world could you have gotten here so quickly?"

"I know it's hard to believe, but we travel in an ASD Transporter and it takes us around the world in minutes," explained Gold.

"ASD?"

"Yes, it stands for Accelerated Speed and Distance, and it allows us to quickly go anywhere there is a problem that needs solving," said Nikko.

"I don't get it," said Patricia. "You're just children. But I do believe you because of what you did in Cuba. Why are you in Capri?"

Gold explained everything from start to finish and when she was done, Patricia saw the hopeless faces of all the kids.

"We have to find a solution," said Cassie.

"I think I can help," said Patricia.

Their faces lit up like multicolored neon signs. They sat quietly waiting to see what she would say, because they were out of options.

"Liana and Otello Berti are friends of mine," said Patricia. "Otello left this morning on a business trip to Rome and his pilot brought me back here to spend a few days with friends. Normally I would be back in Cuba, but since I missed my grandmother's birthday yesterday because of a flight cancellation, I decided to stay. I love Italy.

"Liana did not go to Rome with Otello and is at their villa in Rimini. They have been partners in the business for years, and she can make all the same decisions he can. I will call her, explain everything that happened in Cuba, and tell her I am sending you to see her. Then I will have my private seaplane take you to Rimini to meet her and answer any questions she may have. She trusts me and knows that if I tell her something, it's true. What do you think?"

"I think you're an angel from Heaven," said Eddie, with a grateful sigh.

Patricia laughed and thought this was the least she could do to help the kids who had saved her country from disaster.

She dialed a number on her cell phone but didn't get an answer. "She's probably on the beach right now. I know you don't have much time, so let's go to the port and get you on your way. Don't worry, I'll reach her before you arrive."

"Oh my goodness, thank you so much," said Gold. All the kids hugged her again. They were so happy and grateful.

"But what about the pizzas?" said Eddie. "I'm starving."

"I guess it's going to have to be the candies, little brother," said Gold, leaving money on the table to pay for the pizzas they had ordered. "We'll eat them as soon as we get to the seaplane."

"My limo is here," Patricia said as they

walked to the corner. "We will be at the port in minutes."

The driver got out and opened the back door.

"This is what my life is going to be like when I become a famous magician," Kian whispered to Cassie as they jumped into the back seat.

All the kids were speechless—none of them had ever been inside a limousine before. Patricia couldn't help smiling when she saw how excited they were. They inspected everything from top to bottom in amazement.

"Thank you, thank you, thank you," said Eddie as he and the others jumped around in the back seat.

"You are so very welcome," she said. She was still baffled that kids could do the kinds of things the CLUB US crew did, but she was certain they would be able to help the Bertis.

# CHAPTER 10
(Dieci)
~ dee-eh-chee ~

When they arrived at the port, the chauffeur came around to open the door, and Kian handed him a euro. The chauffeur looked confused.

"That's a tip for you, my friend. I'm practicing because I'll be riding in limousines all the time pretty soon." The kids and Patricia laughed, and so did the chauffeur.

They walked over to the dock where the seaplane was waiting. It was a smaller version of a regular airplane and looked like it was wearing shoes.

"What is a seaplane exactly?" asked Kian.

"It's really cool because it takes off from, and lands on, water," said Nikko. "It's smaller than a regular airplane, but looks very similar except the seaplane has two floats underneath that allow it to sit on the water. It goes a lot farther and faster than a helicopter, and it also holds more people," he continued.

CLUB US could always count on Nikko for an explanation on pretty much everything. It was good to have a nerd on the team.

The plane's motor was running, and the pilot was in the cabin. Patricia had called ahead to let her crew know they were on their way, so everything had been readied for immediate takeoff. The kids couldn't help hugging her one more time, and she loved it.

"When you get to Rimini, the plane will leave you at the port, and you can take a taxi or hitchhike to Liana's villa," said Patricia.

"Hitchhike?" said Cassie. "I don't think so. That's super dangerous."

"Oh, not in Rimini," said Patricia. "Everyone there is so kind and welcoming. People look after each other like one big family. When you arrive at her villa, tell the guard that Patricia Mendéz sent you. I'm going to call Liana now so they will be expecting you. I know you'll do a good job and accomplish your mission. Take care," she said with a huge smile. "Hope to see you again soon!"

The dock attendant closed the door, and the kids took a look at the interior. It was first class all the way, with two long leather couches that ran the entire length of each side of the plane. Right in the middle were pizzas, sodas, and dessert.

"Awesome!" said Cassie. "Thank you, Patricia!" she yelled, as the plane climbed and the city got smaller and smaller. They were on their way to accomplishing their mission and getting home to start spring break.

In the meantime, they all relaxed on the couches eating real Italian pizza.

CHAPTER 11
(Undici)
~ oon-dee-chee ~

The seaplane flew over central Italy and landed in Rimini at six o'clock. As soon as the kids walked down the stairs, they heard music and saw lots of people walking nearby. Rimini already seemed like a fun place, and they hoped they could complete their mission and enjoy some of it before going home. The boardwalk was full of restaurants, cafés, and nightclubs that were preparing for the evening. They bought fresh melon in cups and walked to the main street to find a taxi. It was super busy, and they thought about hitchhiking as Patricia had suggested, when a taxi stopped.

"Ciao!" said Kian as he jumped in the front seat to ride alongside the driver.

"Ciao," said the driver. "Dove state andando ragazzi?"

Kian was ready for a question from him in Italian and held the translator close to his mouth so it could hear him speak.

"Where are you going?" said the translator.

The driver burst into a huge grin when he heard it. "Americani?" he asked with a laugh.

"Si," said Kian, handing him the paper with Liana Berti's address.

The driver took off still laughing about the translator.

There was so much activity on the street. The kids looked from side to side as they rode along and saw one fun thing after the other.

"Look, there's a mime that looks like he's

about nine feet tall," said Cassie.

"Check out his gold metallic suit. Maybe I'll get one like that for my magic act," said Kian with a broad grin.

When the kids looked back over, the mime was standing as still as a statue. Then he moved unexpectantly and everyone around him laughed.

I wonder if I could work that into my act? thought Kian.

There were portrait artists, dancers, jugglers, and people eating and drinking in restaurants along the boulevard.

The driver turned left and followed a tree-lined street that led to a private area with an artistic sign that read COLLE DI COVIGNANO. Once they passed the sign, they saw one enormous villa after another—Villa Ponti, Villa Baldinnini, Villa Franco, and Villa Paci. Then there was one that was so large, they had to drive half a block to see the name, and sure enough, it was Villa Berti. There were guards outside just as Patricia had told them, so they checked the translator to learn how to say "We are Patricia Mendéz's friends" and walked to the gate, prepared for an easy entry.

Gold said, "Buongiorno, siamo gli amici di Patricia Mendéz." She and the others waited for the gates to open.

"Cosa volete?" asked the guard.

Gold quickly repeated "cosa volete" into the translator and heard it say, "What do you want?"

It was obvious the guards had no idea who they were. The sweat started to run down their faces because either Patricia hadn't called her friend Liana, or Liana had not told the guards they were coming.

"Siamo gli amici di Patricia Mendéz, L'amica di Signora Berti," repeated Gold.

"The signora didn't tell us anything, so you're going to have to leave," said another guard from inside the gate.

"At least he speaks English," said Cassie. "Maybe he'll help us."

"Can you please contact Signora Berti? Her friend Patricia Mendéz called from Capri to tell her we were coming. Please," begged Gold.

The guard on the inside of the gate picked up the security phone and called the house. He spoke for a few seconds, then hung up and turned to the kids.

"La signora did not receive a call from Patricia Mendéz today. You will have to leave the property immediately," he said firmly.

The guards outside the gate waved them away, and the crew had no choice but to walk away.

"Now what?" said Cassie. "What are we going to do?"

"I can't believe she didn't call her; something must be wrong," said Gold, twisting her curl. She walked back toward the guards to try and explain again, but they just stood there with their arms crossed, and she knew it was going to be a waste of time.

"OK, guys, let's stay calm. We'll figure something out," said their leader. They headed back to the taxi and got in. They didn't know where to go, but they knew they had to leave Villa Berti.

CLUB US

CHAPTER 12
(Dodici)
~ doh-dee-chee ~

"We have more than twelve hours before we have to meet B.O.R.T.R.O.N., so there's still time," said Gold, as the driver waited for instructions. "What if we call Pierre in Cuba? Maybe he can get in touch with Patricia. There must be some sort of mistake. I'm sure she really wanted to help us."

"Let's do it," said Eddie. "We're wasting time."

"Rimini?" asked the driver.

"Si, grazie," answered Gold.

Just as she pulled out her phone to make the call to Cuba, they saw three young girls waving for the taxi driver to stop. When he did, one of them walked over to the window and said to the kids, "We want to help you."

"Who are you?" asked Cassie.

"We are Liana Berti's daughters."

"And why would you want to help us?" Cassie continued with hesitation.

"We were there when the guard called the house. When she hung up, she wasn't sure if she had made the right decision in telling them to send you away, so she decided to call Patricia. When she reached into her beach bag to grab her phone, it was wet and didn't work. That's why Patricia's call never reached her."

"So that explains it," said Gold.

"Unfortunately, she wasn't able to reach Patricia, so we came to see if there was anything we could do to help. It seems strange that five

CLUB US

American kids would be in Rimini, alone, and we thought you might be in trouble. Who are you, and why are you here?" the girl continued, while smiling at Nikko. It never failed; wherever they went, girls flirted with him.

Nikko looked embarrassed, then softly answered, without looking at any of the sisters. "I'm Nikko. These are my friends Gold, Kian, Eddie, and Cassie. We live in California."

"My name is Valentina, and these are my sisters Kicca and Paola. Nice to meet you."

"But why are you in Rimini? And why do you want to see our mother?" asked Kicca.

"It's complicated, but we'll explain everything to you," said Gold. "Can we go somewhere to talk?"

"Yes, but we can't all fit in this taxi. We will have our driver take us into the city to meet you," said Kicca. She looked through the driver's window and said, "Il Ristorante di Luigi."

"Si, si," said the driver, and he sped off.

The crew arrived at the restaurant and Gold asked for a table for eight by holding up fingers. They were seated outside where they relaxed and waited for the girls to arrive. The sun was setting and the energy was electric.

Within minutes, they heard Paola say "Ciao" to the hostess and point to where the other kids were sitting.

"So, tell us what this is all about," said Valentina, as she and her sisters pulled out chairs and sat with the crew.

"I'll start by saying it will sound crazy, but trust me, it's true," said Gold. "We live in California and we travel around the world in an Accelerated Speed and Distance Transporter to solve life-threatening problems. We are here because your family's company, Berti Motors, is planning to destroy Galotta Automobiles throughout the country."

"What?" said Paola. "That cannot be true. My family would never do anything like that."

"I'm so sorry, Paola, but it is the truth," said Gold. "For the past five years, a number of Berti Motors' employees have digitally infiltrated Galotta Automobile's data center and hacked the computers of all Galotta vehicles. Tomorrow a meltdown of the computers is going to occur, at the same time all over the country. When it happens, every Galotta vehicle—every one—will shut down. I don't have to tell you the devastation that will occur and the lives that will be lost."

"I don't believe you! Come on, Valentina, let's get out of here. They are lying!" said Kicca, standing up to leave the restaurant.

"What are you saying? That can't be," said Valentina, pulling her sister back into her chair.

"I feel awful telling you this, but unfortunately this is what happened, and if we don't do something, people all over the country are going to die."

"Valentina! Do you believe this girl? We don't even know her, or any of these kids," Kicca said, this time with tears in her eyes.

"Kicca, please. Let's hear them out. What if what they're saying is true?"

Kicca sat down once again, but this time with her back to the group. If she had to listen to what they were saying, she didn't want to see their faces.

"But why would my father do such a thing?" asked Valentina.

"If everything goes through as planned," said Gold, "Berti Motors will sell its vehicles to everyone who is a victim of the meltdown, and soon the company will dominate the market. Galotta Automobiles, of course, will be destroyed.

"I wouldn't tell you this if it wasn't true," she continued. "My mom and dad are business owners, and I wouldn't believe some random kids who were telling me such a story about them either. But just hear me out, and then decide.

"When we were first contacted by B.O.R.T.R.O.N. the ASD Transporter, we really couldn't believe what it was telling us. We're sixth graders. Who would ever imagine being able to travel the world at our age to save lives? Our first mission was to Paris, where someone was trying to blow up the Eiffel Tower; our second mission took us to Cuba, where the world's largest volcano was in danger of erupting and destroying the island and everyone on it. This is how we met Patricia Mendéz. Mendéz Oil was the company operating dangerously close to the volcano, and it had to be stopped. If you don't believe me, call her. You know her, so it will be easy, and she'll tell you what we're saying is true."

Valentina thought and thought and finally said, "What can we do?"

CHAPTER 13
(Tredici)
~ treh-dee-chee ~

"Valentina!" screamed her sister. "What are you saying?"

"We have to help them, Kicca. I believe they are telling the truth. Please have faith in me. Have I ever told you anything that was wrong?"

Valentina turned to Gold and asked, "How can we help you?"

"Because our missions only last twenty-four hours, we don't have a lot of time. We need to get to your dad's data center to stop the scheduled meltdown. We thought we could explain the deadly effect of the plot to him, but when we arrived in Capri, he had already left for Rome. This isn't only about stopping the vehicles in the street or preventing them from starting. The meltdown will cause accidents, make it impossible for people to get to the hospital, and prevent police from getting to crime scenes, to name just a few consequences. Because Galotta vehicles are sold all over the country, the damage will be multiplied millions of times," said Gold.

"We tried to explain what was going on to Giancarlo Galotta, but we honestly don't know if he believed us," said Nikko. "We hope he had a chance to think about the proof we showed him, and take steps to stop the people who have infiltrated his data center. Since we're not sure, we must continue our mission, and make sure Berti Motors's computers are shut down in time."

"We were so lucky to run into Patricia,"

continued Gold. "We didn't know what to do when we learned your dad wasn't there, and she told us to come here to talk to your mom. We hoped she would believe us and take the necessary steps to prevent the meltdown."

"Look, Valentina," said Cassie, "we believe your father is a good man, and maybe one day we'll learn why this decision was made, but for now, we have to stop it. Time is running short. Can you go to your mother and explain what's going on? She's the only person that can help us right now."

"Yes! We will do it. Do you have anything I can show her to prove what you're saying is true?" asked Valentina, while Kicca turned to look at the American kids face-to-face. Paola, though quiet, had total confidence in her big sister and was ready to help in any way she could.

Gold handed Valentina the USB drive. "Just tell her to place this drive in her computer and watch the video. When she sees it, it will prove that the threat is real."

Paola walked over to Gold and looked her squarely in the eyes with gratitude. "Thank you. I am certain there is an explanation for this, and one day our papà will give it to us. In the meantime, consider us a part of your team. We will go right now and convince Mamma to help you."

The two girls embraced, and the crew members also gave each of the sisters a sincere hug of appreciation.

"Give me your cell number," said Valentina. "I will call you as soon as we get an answer from Mamma."

"Ciao," said Cassie.

"Ci vediamo," said Paolo as the three sisters got up to leave the restaurant.

"Ci vediamo?" asked Kian.

"See you soon," said Paola.

"Cool," said Kian. "Come on guys, let's check out the city and wait for her call."

CHAPTER 14
(Quattordici)
~ kwaht-tor-dee-chee ~

"Ciao Mamma."

"Ciao bambine," said Liana Berti. Her three girls were each a year apart in age, and they were all so smart and kind. She loved them more than anything in the world, and always enjoyed vacationing with them. They had spent the previous week with their father in Capri, and when he left for a business meeting in Rome, they came to Rimini. Liana was hoping that her husband would join them when the meeting was done.

"Mamma, we have something to tell you," said Paola.

"In English?" laughed their mom. She knew they must want something because they only spoke to her in English to throw her off and put her in a good mood. Liana loved speaking English, but rarely did so in Italy, so she enjoyed practicing with her girls who attended a British school.

"So, what is going to happen?" said Liana.

"Oh Mamma, you mean what's happening," smiled Kicca. They knew speaking to her in English would lighten the mood, and they also knew how important it was to convince her to help the American kids.

"Remember the children who came to the villa earlier today to see you?" asked Paola.

"Si," answered Liana, nodding her head.

"Well, as it turns out they really are friends of Patricia Mendéz, and she sent them here to see you," said Paola. "We kind of heard the

Intrigue in Italy

conversation with the guards, and saw the kids from the window. We were curious and decided to see if we could find them. As they were leaving the villa in a taxi, we agreed to meet up at il Ristorante di Luigi.

"They told us a story that was hard to believe, about our family's company and a plot Papà has to destroy Galotta Automobiles. That's pretty crazy, isn't it, Mamma?"

Liana sat up straight in her leopard-skinned armchair, waiting to hear more.

"It seems Berti Motors has hacked Galotta Automobiles' vehicle computer systems all over the country with a plan to have them all melt down at the same time tomorrow morning. That means people everywhere will be involved in accidents, many of them severe, and millions will die," explained Valentina.

Liana sat frozen in her chair, and it seemed the blood had completely drained from her face.

"Mamma, are you OK?" asked Paola.

"Yes, I am too fine, but I want to see you to stop now," she responded. It was funny hearing their mother speak with her heavy Italian accent and grammatical errors, but at least she was speaking to them in English.

"If you don't believe what I'm saying, let's take a look at the video on the USB drive the American kids gave us," said Paola, handing it to her mother.

"I do believe, figlie," said Liana. "After the children leave, I call my friend Patricia and she explain everything to me," said their mother in a dramatic voice. "I wasn't sure if I do good decision to make these children leave. I don't know them. I know Patricia. Patricia is good friend, too good friend. I ask if she know children, and she tell me yes. She explain all of everything to me. All of *everything*, and I know children tell truth. This terrible thing, it is not your father. He didn't know until I speak to him and tell him. He cry and say he don't know what to do."

Liana also started to cry, which made tears roll down the faces of her three daughters.

"Mamma, what can we do?" asked Paola. "We have to stop it. We don't want people to die."

"We don't want them die too," Liana said between sobs. "Your father call Giancarlo now to tell him he knows nothing of this. He wants to go to data center in Venice but cannot fly until tomorrow because of fog. But we can go there for explain your brother, Mario. The limo wait. Your friends come too. We go together.

"Thank you for finding children," she finished. "Thank you too much, vi amo."

They knew their mother loved them and it made them feel good whenever she told them so, especially now. And in this moment, they were proud of her for doing something to stop the terrible plan.

CHAPTER 15
(Quindici)
~ kween-dee-chee ~

The crew members ate ice cream at Luigi's, then strolled to the main boulevard. There were people everywhere. Couples, families, kids, dogs, artists, entertainers and more. The trees were decorated with blinking white lights, and everyone seemed happy. For blocks and blocks, restaurants and cafés were filled with people enjoying the beautiful evening. Eddie looked in the store windows, while walking, hoping he might find the perfect souvenir for Barks.

Intrigue in Italy

They approached a sign that read ITALIA IN MINIATURA and bought admission tickets. Once inside, the crew walked into a parklike area with a two-block-long boot-shaped display on the ground. They immediately knew it was Italy. As they walked, they saw every Italian city and its most famous monuments. There were hundreds of miniature structures including Trevi Fountain, the Colosseum, the Leaning Tower of Pisa, Venice, and so much more. Only about a foot high each, the details were exactly like the real monuments. The kids saw a Skytrain and hopped on to view the exhibits from overhead. As the train circled the park, they viewed all of the famous landmark sites in Italy, miniature orchestras, airplanes landing and taking off, and lots of miniature people walking the streets.

Just then, Gold's cell phone rang.

"Hello?"

"Gold, this is Valentina. We talked to

Mamma, and she wants to see you. Can you come back?"

"For sure," said Gold. "Come on, guys, let's go. Liana wants to see us."

They jumped off the train at the next stop and ran back to the boulevard to look for a taxi. The streets were full of people, and many of them were waiting for an available taxi to drive by. After at least thirty minutes of holding their hands out to traffic, Gold called Valentina.

"We can't find a taxi, and we're running out of time. Can you meet us here?"

"Yes," said Valentina. "Where are you?"

"We're not far from the restaurant where we met earlier," said Gold. "We'll go back there and wait for you out front."

"Okay, we're on the way."

About fifteen minutes later, a long, black limousine pulled up in front of the restaurant, and the girls lowered the window and beckoned for the crew to join them.

They were glad to see the American kids again, especially Nikko. They thought he was cute, but he was completely oblivious. Being a nerd, he never thought about girls. He was only interested in science and math.

"Mamma is going to help us. Isn't that wonderful?" said Valentina, as the kids jumped into the limo. "She has a plan, but we have to leave immediately to make it happen."

"Where are we going? It's getting late," said Cassie.

"We go to Venice, to explain my son, Mario at data center," said Liana.

"Our brother runs the data center for Berti Motors," said Kicca. "He can stop the meltdown, we just have to get him all the information he needs."

The kids looked at each other and wondered if they could go all the way to Venice, stop the computers, and make it back to B.O.R.T.R.O.N. in time.

"How far is Venice?" asked Cassie.

"Not far. Let's go," said Valentina.

CHAPTER 16
(Sedici)
~ seh-dee-chee ~

It was dark and foggy, so they didn't see much on the road to Venice. The crew members were hungry and took out their translators to eat some of their multicolored 'food'. They opened the drawers and first pointed them in the direction of the Berti family.

"Try one," said Kian. "They're good!"

Liana shook her head. She tried not to eat candy—ever.

Her daughters, on the other hand, reached

in and grabbed a couple of the chocolate-filled sweets—or so they thought. Valentina popped a brown one in her mouth and exclaimed, "What!? This tastes like a hamburger."

"And mine tastes like a cheeseburger," said Paola. "How is that possible? That's crazy."

"I know it's hard to believe, but it's all a part of our mission," said Kian. "I'm going for the red one to see if it tastes as good as the pizza we had on the seaplane. I doubt it, but who knows," he said as he popped the red candy into his mouth.

"What is happen?" asked Liana.

"Try one, Mamma. They taste like food," said Paola.

Her curiosity won out and Liana tried a yellow candy. They were right; it tasted just like french fries. She laughed and said, "Pazzo!"

"That means 'crazy' in Italian," said Kicca.

They all laughed and everyone started burping from the sodas that came with their choices.

CHAPTER 17
(Diciasette)
~ dee-chahs-set-teh ~

When they arrived, they didn't see the big canal they had read about in geography class.

"Where's the water?" asked Eddie. "I thought that's what this city was all about."

"You'll see soon enough," said Kicca. They exited the limousine and walked over to a train station.

"A train station in Venice?" asked Cassie.

"To get from the airport to the city, we must take a train," said Valentina. "It's only two stops.

CLUB US

We will be there in a few minutes."

When they walked out of the station, their eyes fell on the immense Grand Canal, which ran through the center of Venice. It looked like the photographs they had seen in their schoolbooks, but so much bigger than they ever imagined.

Side by side, they walked down the wide staircase to the dock, where there was a boat waiting. The captain greeted them with a smile and "Buonasera" as they approached. The boat was big enough for ten people and was enclosed with wood so shiny the kids could see their reflections. Stepping onboard, they saw red velvet couches and gold accents everywhere. An elegant woman welcomed them and offered everyone a bottle of water with the name Berti on the label. This was luxury at its best.

In the middle of the boat was an ornate table with Italian desserts and one glass of champagne, for Liana. The captain took off smoothly and everyone looked out the windows onto the canal. They saw gondolas with loving couples and gondoliers singing them romantic ballads as they rowed the vessels in a standing position, small private boats, and waterbuses full of people. The water was black and sparkled with the lights shining from the buildings on the right and left.

They rode under bridges, and Gold suddenly remembered being there when she was a tiny girl. "I think that's the Rialto Bridge," she said. "Eddie was still in a stroller, do you remember Eddie?"

Eddie gave her a blank stare. He wanted to say he did, but instead responded, "Who remembers what happened when they were in a stroller? Anybody here?"

They all laughed.

"I think there's also a place here with lots and lots of pigeons," said Gold. "We visited when I was a toddler."

"St. Mark's Square," said Nikko. "It's a

CLUB US

popular place and sometimes floods because it's the lowest part of the city."

"Smart boy," said Liana, turning to her girls and smiling.

Cute too, the girls all thought.

Liana was so grateful these children had been sent to her, and that her girls had ventured out to find them.

She wondered who would want to destroy Galotta Automobiles and hurt so many people in the process. She knew her husband would make sure that whoever it was would be punished, but first she needed to stop it from happening.

They continued down the canal until the city of Venice started to disappear behind them. Soon they found themselves in open waters. Only minutes passed before a much smaller island came into view. The captain docked the boat, and they could see three young men waiting.

As they disembarked, one of the men walked

over to Liana and gave her a kiss on both cheeks. He also kissed the three girls, and said hello to the CLUB US crew.

"Welcome to Santa Cristina. I'm Mario, as you can probably tell," he smiled. "I'm here to help in any way I can. My sisters and mother explained the situation, and we were all shocked by it. There is no way our family would ever do something like this to the Galottas. My father worked with Giancarlo more than fifty years ago, and even though they opened separate businesses, they've always respected one another.

"We've done some investigation since yesterday, and it looks like we've also been infiltrated," said Mario. "Let me introduce you to my assistants, Michelangelo and Carlo."

"Hello," said Carlo, reaching out to shake their hands with a look of pain on his face. "I don't know everything yet, but there is a foreign automobile manufacturer who devised an elaborate scheme to destroy Galotta Automobiles... and us."

There was a gasp from the Berti family and the CLUB US crew. Even B.O.R.T.R.O.N. hadn't been aware of the depth of the plan and thought that Otello Berti was behind the potential destruction of Galotta.

As they walked to the data center, Michelangelo continued. "We confirmed that the foreign company has infiltrated Galotta Automobiles' factories throughout the country. As you know, hackers have orchestrated a coordinated meltdown of all Galotta vehicles tomorrow morning, and because the outside company wants it to appear that this plan was initiated by an Italian competitor, they paid off members of our team to help them put it into action. We were devastated to learn that some of our most trusted technicians have been on the infiltrators' payroll for the past five years and have worked with them to initiate the meltdown from our center. Once the damage has been done, the foreign company will buy Giancarlo <u>and</u> Otello out. Their reputations will be saved; however, these old friends will lose everything they've worked all their lives for.

"If we don't stop the meltdown, lives and careers throughout Italy, including ours, will be destroyed," said Carlo.

"It's a lot to take in," said Mario. "We will learn more in the next few days, but for now we have to stop the plan."

"Here is the video that will explain exactly how they have reconfigured the computers to schedule the mass meltdown," said Gold, handing Mario the USB drive. Even though they now understood the plan was even grander than they'd realized, the procedure explained on the drive was what they still needed to follow to stop the devastation.

Mario, Michelangelo, and Carlo headed to the data center. The others followed.

Once inside, they went into Mario's office to watch the video. They were saddened to think Otello, and his friend Giancarlo, had been victims of this plan. They printed the documents that were on the drive, and laid everything out on the table to carefully examine. They spoke with each other rapidly, and after about ten minutes, Mario gave the crew members and his family a condensed version of what they discussed.

"This isn't going to be easy. It's more complicated than we thought. In order for it to work, we need our team in Milan to manage the control panel and push the disabling buttons at the same time that we do here. Carlo has gone to call them."

Mario looked worried, and of course, everyone picked up on it.

"Will he be able to reach them so late?" asked Nikko.

"We don't know. That's what we are hoping,"

said Mario.

Finally, Carlo returned to the group. "I was able to reach a member of our team. He is on his way to the main programmer's house to let him know what's going on, because he is not answering the phone. We need this programmer to control the process in Milan."

"OK, let's get things moving on our end and hope he will be able to find him and start the process in Milan," said Mario. "This is going to be a matter of precise teamwork from both of our data centers."

They headed to the room that housed the immense setup of servers that ran twenty-four hours a day.

"Will you have to shut them all down?" asked Gold.

"No, just the ones that are linked to the computer systems in the vehicles," responded Michelangelo. "Once we get into the main computer, we can easily identify which ones must be disabled and get it done quickly.

"Since the backups are in the Milan office, for security purposes, we must work hand in hand," said Carlo as he walked the room, eyes darting from server to server, then down to the documents in his hands.

There wasn't much they could do until they heard back from Milan. They all tried to make small talk, but everyone was so nervous it was hard to converse. Finally, the telephone rang.

"Pronto," said Mario, putting his cell phone to his ear. "Si, si, nessun problema."

"So, we're good to go?" asked Gold.

"No, that was my wife, reminding me to bring home milk for my sons, Mario Jr. and Biaggio."

If it wasn't so scary, they would have laughed. But at this moment, laughter wasn't something anyone could muster.

Finally the call they had been waiting for

Intrigue in Italy

came in. Mario spoke quickly because there was so much information to share with his team. They heard him say, "Bene, bene! Lo faremo esattamente alle 6:40. Grazie!"

"Is everything OK?" asked Valentina.

"Yes, we are going to stop the computers that control the vehicle systems in both locations at exactly 6:40 a.m."

As he hung up the phone he further explained. "Davide was able to find the programmer, and they are now at the Milan data center. We discussed exactly what needs to be done, and they are prepared. Now we must get to work here. I'll be right back, and I promise you it will be fine." He dashed away with a look of determination, and concern, on his face.

"Awesome!" said Cassie. She and Kian hugged. Gold reminded them, "Don't get too excited. We have to wait to see if they can do it first."

They heard a soft voice from the other side of the room and turned to see Liana with her eyes closed and her fingers moving through her rosary beads.

"Mamma is praying to Saint Joseph, who protects people from harm," said Kicca. They left her alone and waited for an update from the team.

# CHAPTER 18
(Diciotto)
~ dee-choht-toh ~

Mario had run into a glitch on his end. He was certain his team could stop the plan put into place by the infiltrators, but at the moment, nothing was falling into place. Carlo and Michelangelo continued working furiously with the team in Milan, and Mario went back to the office to update the crew members and his family.

"We've run into a problem," he said with a sigh. "We can't seem to get the—" Before he could finish his sentence, the entire data center went dark. The machines stopped running and the only thing that could be seen in both rooms were wide-eyed stares.

Somebody, please tell me I'm dreaming. thought Cassie. *Without electricity, it won't be possible to complete the mission.* No one moved or said a word. The only sound was Liana's rosary beads moving even more quickly through her fingers.

"Mario," Valentina finally said, pleadingly. Before another word came out of her mouth, the lights flickered, and they heard the hum of the computers revving back up. Mario looked through the small window between the office and the data control room and saw his assistants giving him two thumbs-up.

The CLUB US crew and the Berti girls screamed with joy and relief, then jumped on top of Mario to give him a group hug of gratitude. Liana looked at them from the corner of her eye and continued praying until Valentina walked over and said, "Va bene, Mamma, va bene."

And even though Cassie joined in the celebration, she couldn't help asking Mario, "Are you sure? How can you guarantee the meltdown won't still occur in the morning?"

"Our technicians are among the best in the world, and all the indicators on the control panels assure us that their plan has been foiled. Tomorrow at seven, traffic will run as smoothly as it does every morning. The people of Italy are safe, and it's all thanks to you," he continued, looking at the crew. "Grazie. Mille grazie!"

CHAPTER 19
(Diciannove)
~ dee-chahn-noh-veh ~

They walked back to the waiting boat thanking Mario and his team along the way. Liana had put away her rosary and was also smiling and happy with the outcome.

"Mio figlio é molto intelligente," said Liana with pride.

"Inglese, Mamma," said Kicca.

"Oh yes, my son is very intelligent," she responded in perfect English, with a huge smile of pride.

"Bravo, Mamma, you are right!" said Paola.

Everyone said goodbye, then Liana, her daughters, and the CLUB US crew stepped down into the boat. They headed back toward Venice and pulled into the dock of a building that looked like a castle. The lighting on the exterior was golden amber, and the red, white, and green Italian flag that waved proudly above the entrance, demonstrated the national pride the owners took in their property.

Liana spoke to her daughters and asked them to translate.

"My mother wants you to know that this is the Gritti Palace, one of the nicest hotels in Venice, and where we will sleep tonight."

"What time will we leave in the morning?" asked Cassie.

Liana understood her and said, "Eight o'clock."

"Oh no, that's too late. We must be back at the Trevi Fountain in Rome by 8:27."

The girls explained to their mother, who thought for a second.

"OK," she said, "we leave hotel five-thirty. You fly Rome in Otello's private plane six o'clock. Plane in Rome seven ten. You at Trevi at eight. OK?"

Nikko quickly responded, "Si, Signora! Molto OK!"

# CHAPTER 20
(Venti)
~ ven-tee ~

One by one, they stepped off the boat. They all said "Grazie" to the captain and he answered "Prego." It was always good to know thank you and you're welcome in another language.

They glanced up and saw the full moon shining brightly against the black sky. Looking down the length of the canal, they could see all the beautifully lit buildings they had just passed. And even though they knew Venice was sinking little by little each year, the amazing night view they witnessed was something they would never, ever forget.

They followed Liana across a narrow bridge to the entrance of the hotel. On the left was a small restaurant where people were finishing a late dinner on a floating terrace. As they approached the glamorous hotel, the huge glass entrance doors were swung open by two doormen who greeted them.

"Benvenuto, Signora Berti," they said.

Liana and the girls smiled and said, "Grazie," and the CLUB US members followed their lead. The crew was very excited, because everyone treated them like royalty.

The lobby looked like the living room of a rich person's home. There were plush chairs, couches, and marble floors, and on the walls was the kind of art they thought only existed in museums. Every table and counter had colorful bouquets of flowers in expensive-looking vases, and there were people dusting and tidying up every surface.

Eddie yanked the bottom of Kian's T-shirt. "Look! Isn't that—?"

Before he could finish, the gorgeous woman turned and smiled at them. She then entered the elevator and the doors closed before they could ask for an autograph.

"Oh. My. God," said Kian. "I can't believe it was really her!"

Just then, a man with a sincere smile, appeared.

"Buonasera, Signora Berti. Benvenuto." He looked at her as though she was a queen, and she certainly appeared, and acted, like one.

"Buonasera, Marcello," said Liana. They walked together to a small desk where four keys were waiting for them. Paola gave one to Gold and Cassie and one to Eddie, Kian, and Nikko; she kept the other two. "Our suites are on the top," she said. "Let's get fresh, then meet on roof in one hour."

"She means top floor, freshen up and meet on the rooftop," laughed Paola.

The kids loved hearing Liana speak English. She was certain she spoke it perfectly and didn't think it was necessary to make any changes—at all. She was great!

They rode up in the elevator together and got off on the top floor. Once again, everything was elegant and expensive looking. The walls had antique-looking light fixtures, and there was exquisite art everywhere.

"These are your suites," said Valentina. "Numbers 408 and 409. We are in 410 and my mother is in 418. We'll see you on the rooftop in an hour."

The boys entered their suite and screamed in surprise. There were mirrored doors, cabinets and tables, fabric wall coverings, and chandeliers. Like downstairs, fresh flowers in glass vases were everywhere, as well as statues and artwork. They turned on the eighty-inch flatscreen television that spoke to them in Italian, then went into the white marble bathroom to check it out.

"This is epic!" exclaimed Eddie. "Am I dreaming?"

"No, you're not, buddy. Get used to it, because this is exactly how I'll be traveling when I get famous, and you'll all be right there with me."

They were interrupted by a knock at the door. It was the girls.

"Oh my goodness, they have the same room as we do, only bigger," said Gold.

"Well, there's three of us and only two of you, so of course our *suite*—not *room*, sis—should be bigger," said Eddie. "Plus, they probably know Kian is a future celebrity, so they wanted to impress him," he continued with a laugh.

"Check this out," said Nikko, leading them into a second bedroom that was just as amazing as everything else in the suite.

"I could live like this right now," said Kian. "Are you sure you guys want to go home?"

"Yes!" said Cassie, then flashed a smile.

She and Gold returned to their suite and relaxed in the living room. They watched a bit of television in Italian, then decided to head on up to the rooftop to meet Liana and the girls. When they passed the boys' suite, they knocked and Gold said, through the door, "C'mon guys, it's time to go."

Kian pushed the UP button on the elevator and when the doors opened on the rooftop, they weren't surprised to enter a gorgeous lounge with white leather chairs and couches throughout the space. The rooftop view of Venice was breathtaking, and even though it was very late, they saw small islands everywhere.

"What are all those islands?" asked Eddie.

"There are one hundred and twenty of them and they are all a part of the city of Venice," said

Valentina. "There are also over four hundred bridges and we have to cross some of them every day. It's a great place to visit, but lots and lots of walking because cars cannot drive here and sometimes boats aren't available."

They heard the 'ding' of the elevator and when the door opened, Liana stepped out looking even more regal than she had earlier in the day.

They joined her at a grouping of couches, and the waiter brought over snacks and soft drinks. Of course, Liana had her usual glass of champagne.

"Remember we wake very, very early. . . four-thirty is good," said Liana. "Breakfast will come to room, because too early for restaurant. My boat wait for us to go to airport. Va bene?"

"Do you have any questions?" asked Paola.

"Yes, are there any pizzas at this hotel?" asked Kian. "I'm still hungry."

"Certamente!" said Liana. "Cameriere, pizzas per favore."

"Si, Signora," said the waiter. "Subito!"

Eddie pulled out the translator and repeated "Subito." It said, "immediately." When the kids heard that, they grinned.

While waiting, they talked about the danger, and fun, they had experienced in Italy. The Berti girls joined in, as did their mother. . .mostly in Italian, and everyone relaxed feeling certain the mission had been successful.

Soon the pizzas arrived and everyone grabbed slices of their favorites.

"These are so much better than at home," said Gold.

"Well, they should be. You're in Italy!" said Paola with a laugh.

~ ~ ~

"Well, guys, we did it," said Gold as the group stepped out of the elevator on the fourth floor. "Now we just have to get to the airport on time to fly back to Rome."

"Get some sleep. We'll see you in the lobby at five o'clock. Buona notte, good night," said Kicca as they opened the doors to their suites. When no one was looking, she winked at Nikko, and his face turned as red as a tomato.

CHAPTER 21
(Venti oo-no)
~ ven-tee oo-noh ~

The alarm clock rang at four o'clock in Eddie, Kian, and Nikko's suite. No one moved. It continued ringing, but the boys didn't budge. They heard knocking on the wall next door and realized it was the girls telling them it was time to get up.

Kian cupped his hands to the wall and said, "OK, OK."

They heard one last light knock that confirmed the girls had heard him. It was totally black outside their window. The sun wouldn't rise for a couple of hours, but they knew they had to get going long before it peeked its head over the horizon.

Just then a doorbell rang.

"A doorbell in a hotel room? Come in!" Kian said, making a note for his travel requirements when he became famous.

"Must be the girls," said Eddie, brushing his teeth with the toothbrush provided by the hotel. Nikko opened the door and a long table entered filled with all kinds of breakfast items. At the end of the table was a smiling waiter dressed in a white uniform and a chef's hat. He just stood there smiling with pride at the beautiful array of breakfast foods that had been prepared for them. Liana had instructed the kitchen to have something delivered to their suites early, and the layout included fruit, cereal, bacon and eggs, juices, pastries, pancakes, and lobster omelettes. They were amazed.

"Grazie, grazie!" said Nikko.

"Prego!" said the waiter. He waved goodbye

and closed the door. The boys sat down at the dining table and filled themselves with delicious food.

Afterward they washed their faces, then sadly left the suite. It was almost five o'clock. As the elevator door was closing, they heard the girls coming down the hall. Nikko held the door open and they all went down together.

"This place is getting better and better," said Eddie as they walked into the lobby. "That was one of the best breakfasts I've ever had."

Within seconds the elevator door opened again and the Berti girls exited, followed by their very special mom.

"Buongiorno," said Liana.

"Buongiorno o buona notte?" asked Nikko with a smile. He wasn't sure if she meant good morning or good evening. It was still nighttime outside, but the morning had begun, and they were approaching one of the most important parts of their mission.

The lobby was empty apart from the nine of them and Marcello, who was waiting to say goodbye.

"Molto grazie, Signora," he said and smiled at the whole group as they walked outside. They waved at him, and he waved back. They were sorry to leave the over-the-top hotel, and as in Paris and Cuba, hoped one day they would return.

The private boat was once again waiting, and the same captain who had brought them there last night greeted them.

Valentina and Paola explained to him that they needed to get to the private airport as quickly as possible. He rapidly turned the boat to the canal and sped off, leaving a wake behind them. Tommaso was an experienced driver and knew how to maneuver the waters of the Grand Canal. He had been driving boats there all his life and had been with the Berti family for decades.

"Tommaso is an amazing captain," said Kicca. "He will get us there on time."

The sun was beginning to rise and the contrast against the water was breathtaking. Since there were very few boats on the canal besides theirs, the water was calm and still. Unfortunately, the CLUB US crew members were much too nervous to appreciate it. Even though they believed Mario and his team had been successful, they still worried what might happen at seven o'clock.

Valentina realized how nervous they were, so she took out her cell phone and called the pilot. "We'll be there in seven minutes. Please be ready for takeoff," she said.

Tommaso continued to steer the boat as fast and carefully as he could, and soon they saw the airport in sight. He pulled up to the dock and the kids jumped off and rushed toward the plane. The motor of the Berti family's Cessna was running, and the pilot was waiting outside.

"Oh my goodness, how can we ever thank you?" Gold asked the Berti girls. "We never could have done this without the three of you. Thank you, thank you, thank you!!!"

"And thank you all for what you do for our family and for Italy. Now get on plane and go!" said Liana, shooing them to the plane.

Just as they approached the stairs, two men walked down to meet them. They recognized Giancarlo and hoped he wasn't still angry.

"Grazie, ragazzi!" he said with a deep laugh and huge smile. He put his cigar down for a moment and gave them all a big hug. "You saved our lives!"

Otello held each of the children's hands and with a tear in his eye said, "How can we thank you? If you ever need anything from me or from Giancarlo, we're here for you."

They kids were happy and waved goodbye to everyone from the top of the stairs. The door closed, and before they could even get their seat belts on, they were lifting off.

They continued to wave from the window and when Nikko looked out, he saw all three of the Berti girls throw him a kiss. He was so embarrassed he almost slid under the seat.

CHAPTER 22
(Ventidue)
~ ven-tee-doo-eh ~

Soon they saw the city of Rome come into view. The Vatican, the Forum, the Spanish Steps and the Colosseum were even more impressive from above, and seeing Trevi Fountain made them more anxious than ever to get back there. The Cessna landed smoothly at Rome Ciampino Airport, and before the pilot took off his headphones and seatbelt, the kids were standing at the exit door. Within seconds, they ran down the stairs and across the tarmac to the main building. As soon

CLUB US

as they walked through the glass doors, they saw the gorgeous woman from the hotel going up the escalator.

"Oh my gosh!! It's totally her!" said Kian. She knew they recognized her because she waved and blew them a kiss before she reached the second floor. "I wish we could have gotten her autograph," Kian sighed.

"No worries, buddy," said Eddie. "You'll probably be best friends once you become a famous magician, and we can get it then."

"You're right Eddie," said Kian as he waved goodbye to her, then ran out the front door with the others to grab a taxi. The oversized clock at the taxi stand said 7:10, and the crew jumped for joy seeing all the vehicles at the airport operating as they always did. The meltdown had been foiled!

"Trevi Fountain," Kian told the taxi manager. The manager waved over the first taxi in line and conveyed their destination to the driver. They squeezed into the mid-sized car. *Where was a van when you needed one?*, thought Cassie.

Gold took out her translator. "How long will it take us to get to Trevi Fountain?" she said into the machine. The driver started the car, and she touched his shoulder to stop him from taking off. She then put the translator near his face and pushed the *Play* button as he slammed on the brakes.

He heard, "Quanto tempo ci vorrà per arrivare a la Fontana di Trevi?"

"Un'ora e venti minuti."

The translator said, "An hour and twenty minutes."

"Oh no," said Cassie. "The sign inside the airport said forty minutes."

The taxi manager popped his head inside the passenger window and asked with irritation, "Cosa sta succedendo? What's going on?"

Gold opened the door and stood outside the car to explain. "We must be at Trevi Fountain in forty minutes. The driver says it will take nearly an hour and a half."

"It's rush hour, and there's a lot of traffic—just look," he said, pointing to the freeway outside the airport. "Of course, it's going to take longer."

By then everyone had jumped out of the taxi. "Cosa sta succedendo?" asked the driver.

The manager pointed to the next passengers in line and waved them over. Two ladies in business suits hopped in, and the driver sped off.

"There's another way to get to Trevi faster at this time of day, and it is the underground Metro," said the taxi manager. He pointed to the left of the stand and continued, "Do you see the red sign in front of the next building?"

"Yes," said Gold.

"Inside the door are stairs that will take you to the lower level. You'll see the train for Rome straight ahead. It will get you there much faster than a taxi—hurry!"

Intrigue in Italy

"Grazie!" they yelled, speeding toward the red sign. They entered the building, flew down the steps, and in front of them was a waiting train that said ROMA. The kids looked at the line in front of the ticket machine, then at each other. Without saying a word, they all jumped over the turnstile and ran toward the train. On their heels was a Metro Polizia yelling "Fermatevi!" As the train doors started closing, the crew jumped on and hid in the crowd.

Twenty-five minutes later, the train arrived at the Barberini-Fontana di Trevi train station. The kids bolted up the stairs to the street and saw the amazing fountain. They threw one last coin in, over their left shoulder, then entered the hotel.

"Buongiorno," said the clerk at the desk. "May I help you?"

"Yes, we are guests of the hotel," said Eddie.

The clerk looked at them with a quizzical expression. "Where are your parents?"

"They are still asleep, so we walked over to throw a coin in the fountain."

She knew he wasn't telling the truth. She had been there all morning and had not seen anyone leave the hotel.

"I'm going to call security; you need to talk to them," she said, picking up the telephone.

"Now what?" Cassie whispered to Gold.

"Let's get out of here. If security comes, we're going to be in big trouble."

The kids raced out the front door while the receptionist was talking. They heard her yell, "Fermatevi!" and so did the Polizia outside the door.

They ran around to the back of the hotel to see if there was another way in. There were two doors, but both were locked. Suddenly, one of the doors opened as a worker came out to throw away a bag of trash. When he turned his back, they snuck inside and found themselves in the hotel kitchen. Just in time, as the Polizia were rounding the corner of the hotel.

Cooks were prepping food for the day, making coffee, squeezing fruit for juice, and baking pastries for the hotel guests' morning meal. The kids hid in a dark corner and Eddie noticed a door that led to a back hallway. "C'mon guys," he said.

In the hallway, was a door marked SCALE with a graphic of a flight of stairs. The door was locked ...of course.

Gold looked at her cell phone. It was 8:19 and B.O.R.T.R.O.N. was leaving at 8:27. She had an idea. She walked over to the door, banged on it, then hid around the corner with the other kids. She hoped someone in the kitchen would think a co-worker was stuck on the other side. It worked. An employee opened the door but didn't see anyone. Thinking he was hearing things, he hunched his shoulders and walked back into the kitchen. When he did, the kids rushed from their hiding spot and Cassie stuck her foot between the door and the frame to keep it from closing. They all ran out and up the stairs as fast as they could. When they reached the roof, they heard B.O.R.T.R.O.N.'s motor revving. They dashed toward the transporter to board, then remembered they needed to shrink. Circle. Fingers to middle. Touch. Boom! Within seconds they were back to travel size and ran on board.

CHAPTER 23
(Ventitré)
~ ven-tee-treh ~

"You guys must be kidding me," said the screen.

CHAPTER 24
(Ventiquattro)
~ ven-tee kwaht-troh ~

"But B.O.R.T.R.O.N.," said Kian. "This one was crazier than ever!"

"No excuses," said the transporter. "You're supposed to be getting better and better at this, and you're getting worse and worse. You literally had seconds left before takeoff. You can't keep doing this."

The kids felt awful. B.O.R.T.R.O.N. was right. They were really cutting it way too close. If they had arrived one minute later, they would have had to figure out how to get home on their own. They didn't know what to say. The screen turned black and the only sound was the hum of the transporter's motor.

Suddenly, the screen lit up.

"I hope I scared you guys," B.O.R.T.R.O.N. laughed. "You did an amazing job, and you're here—that's what's most important. But I beg of you, DO NOT SCARE ME LIKE THAT AGAIN!"

"We won't, B.O.R.T.R.O.N.. We promise!" they all said.

On the way home there was so much chatter it was hard for B.O.R.T.R.O.N. to keep up.

"Would you believe there was a foreign automobile manufacturer behind the scheme?" said Eddie.

"And they had planned to destroy both Giancarlo Galotta *and* Otello Berti!" continued Cassie.

B.O.R.T.R.O.N. wasn't aware of that and

was pleased to know that the kids had stepped up to a challenge they weren't expecting.

"You'll have to tell me more about that when we land," said B.O.R.T.R.O.N.. "Did you enjoy Italy?"

"Yes! I loved the fountain," said Cassie, "even though I threw my coin over the wrong shoulder."

"Right," said Nikko with a grin. "And that's when our troubles began."

"For me the funniest part was when we hid in the bushes of the convent. . . twice!" said Kian. "The nuns didn't understand what was going on, but they protected us when we needed it and wished us good luck with a smile."

"I was blown away by Pompeii. The people and animals in the glass display boxes who had been covered by ash and lava were epic," said Eddie. "They looked like statues."

"For me the best part was the pizzas," said

Kian. "They were the best ever!"

"I loved riding in Liana's luxurious boat on the canal in Venice. The only boats I had ever seen in the movies about Venice were the gondolas, but hers was to die for," said Gold. "What about you, Nikko? What was your favorite part?"

"I know!" said Kian. "It was when the three sisters were making goo-goo eyes at you in Rimini. 'Nikko, you're so cute,'" he mocked.

All the kids laughed at that one, and Nikko was embarrassed again. At the same time, it made him feel good that girls thought he was cute. That was something he never expected to hear in his life, and he joined the others in laughter.

"Well, we're almost there," said B.O.R.T.R.O.N.. "Thank you all for such an amazing job. Don't ever forget, you saved millions of lives all over Italy."

"And we had fun doing it," said Kian.

CHAPTER 25
(Venticinque)
~ ven-tee-cheen-kweh ~

"We're back, Mr. Smith," said Eddie as the kids ran into Mr. Smith's living room. Their friend had fallen asleep awaiting their arrival, so he was surprised they had already landed and grown back to normal size.

As always, Barks was excited and jumped around giving limitless sloppy kisses to all his friends. He stood at Eddie's feet, tail wagging, waiting for more hugs from his best bud.

"Hey, Barks, just like I promised, I have a

souvenir for you," Eddie said, reaching into his pocket.

"When did you have time to buy a souvenir?" asked Gold.

"Aha! Never underestimate a fourth grader," laughed Eddie, handing Barks his brand-new Roman gladiator dog bone.

"Well, Mr. Smith, we're heading home now," said Gold.

"We're so tired, we're probably going to sleep through the first two days of spring break," laughed Eddie.

"I don't blame you. When you're rested up, we'll have to get together so I can hear all about your adventure."

"You got it, Mr. Smith!" said Eddie as he and the other crew members ran home. They felt like the luckiest kids in the whole world.

CLUB US

Grazie!

Mille grazie for taking an exciting trip with
us to Italy! We hope you also enjoyed both
Peril in Paris and Crisis in Cuba,
and will take a sneak peek
at the excerpt of Evil in Egypt
in the back of this book.

We would also be so grateful if you, or the
adult that bought you this book, would
leave us a review on our Amazon page
so others can see what you thought
about the adventure.
JUST DON'T GIVE AWAY THE ENDING!

Thanks again from all of us!
Gold, Nikko, Cassie, Kian, Eddie
Mr. Smith, Barks & B.O.R.T.R.O.N.

GLOSSARY

Speaking a foreign language is lots of fun, though it's important to remember that many sounds in other languages don't exist in English. This phonetic guide will make it easy to pronounce words in Italian, and if you follow the three tips below, you'll soon be speaking the language like a pro!

#1: Pronounce the words in parentheses. Your pronunciation will be more accurate.

#2: When pronouncing the words, always put the accent on the syllable that is underlined.

#3: Whenever you see a hyphenated pronunciation, remember it represents just one word.

A che ora parte il prossimo aliscafo?
(ah kay oh-ra par-tay eel pros-ee-moe a-lees-ca-foe)

What time does the next hydrofoil leave?

Allora, andiamo!
(ah-lor-ah ahn-dee-ah-moe)

So, let's go!

Americani
(ah-mair-ee-kan-ee)

Americans

Arrivederci
(ah-ree-veh-dare-chee)

Good-bye

Bambini 　　　　　　　　Children
(bahm-bean-ee)

Bene, molto bene 　　　　Good, very good
(ben-ay, mol-to ben-ay)

Bene, bene lo faremo 　　Good, good we will
essattamente alle 6:40 　do it exactly at 6:40
*(ben-ay, ben-ay, loh
fah-ray-moe
es-sat-tah-men-tay ah-lay
say-ees kwa-ran-ta)*

Benvenuto 　　　　　　　Welcome
(ben-ven-oo-toe)

Biglietti 　　　　　　　　Tickets
(big-lee-et-tee)

Buona notte 　　　　　　Good night
(bwon-ah no-tay)

Buonasera 　　　　　　　Good evening
(bwon-ah-sair-ah)

Buongiorno 　　　　　　Good day or
(bwon-jorn-oh) 　　　　Good morning

Buongiorno bambini 　　Good day children,
cosa ci fate qui? 　　　　what are you doing
*(bwon-jorn-noe 　　　　here?
bahm-bean-ee kosa
chee fah-tay kwee)*

Buongiorno siamo gli amici di Patricia Mendéz
(bwon-jorn-noe see-ah-moe yee ah-mee-chee dee pah-tree-see-ah men-dez)
We are friends of Patricia Mendéz

Cameriere
(kah-mair-ee-air-ay)
Waiter

Certamente
(cher-ta-men-tay)
Sure/of course

Chiuso
(kee-oo-so)
Closed

Ci vediamo
(chee-vee-dee-ah-moe)
See you later

Ciao amici
(chow ah-mee-chee)
Hi friends

Ciao ragazzi
(chow rah-gahz-zee)
Hi guys

Ciao sorella
(chow sor-rell-ah)
Hi sisters

Cinquanta euro
(cheen-kwan-tah eh-oo-roe)
Fifty euros

Cosa sta succedendo? *(koh-sa sta soo-che-den-doe)*	What's going on?
Cosa volete? *(koh-sa vo-leh-tay)*	What do you want?
Dove state andando? *(doh-vay stah-tey ahn-dan-doe)*	Where are you going?
Dove vanno? *(doh-vay van-o)*	Where are you going?
Duecento venticinque euro *(do-ay-chen-toe ven-tee-cheen-kway eh-oo-roe)*	Two hundred and twenty-five euros
Fermatevi! *(fair-mah-teh-vee)*	Stop!
Figlie *(feel-yee)*	Daughters
Gelateria *(je-lah-tair-ee-ah)*	Ice cream store
Gelato *(je-lah-toe)*	Ice cream
Grazie *(grah-zee-ay)*	Thank you

Il Ristorante di Luigi
*(eel rees-toe-ran-tay
dee loo-ee-jee)*

Luigi's Restaurant

Il Signor Berti non
è qui e non tornerà
per tre giorni.
*(eel sig-nore bair-tee
non eh kwee eh non
torn-air-ah pair tray
jee-or-nee)*

Mr. Berti is not here
and he won't be back
for three days.

L'amica de Signora
Berti
*(lah-mee-kah dee
sig-nor-ah bair-tee)*

Mrs. Berti's friend

Mio figlio é molto
intelligente
*(mee-oh feel-ee-o
eh mol-toe inteli-hen-tay)*

My son is very
intelligent

Non può portare
questi bambini
*(non pwo por-tar-ay
kwes-tee bahm-bean-ee)*

You can't take these
these children

Ora andate a trovare
i vostri amici
*(or-ah ahn-da-tay ah
tro-vah-ray ee
vos-tree ah-mee-chee)*

Now go and find
your friends

Pazzo *(pahz-zo)*	Crazy
Per favore *(pair fah-vore-ay)*	Please
Pizzeria *(pee-zair-ee-ah)*	Pizza restaurant
Polizia *(po-lee-zee-ah)*	Police
Portineria *(por-tee-nair-ee-ah)*	Lobby
Prego *(pray-go)*	You're welcome
Prima Classe *(pree-mah klas-say)*	First Class
Pronto *(prawn-toe)*	Hello (telephone)
Quanto tempo ci vorrà per arrivare a la Fontana di Trevi? *(kwan-toe tem-poe chee vo-rah pair ahree-vah-ray ah lah fon-tah-na dee tre-vee?)*	How long will it take us to arrive at Trevi Fountain?

San Guiseppe vi proteggerà *(sahn je-<u>sep</u>-ay vee pro-tegg-air-<u>ah</u>)*	Saint Joseph will protect you
State ancora giocando con i vostri amici? *(<u>sta</u>-tay ahn-<u>kor</u>-ah jee-oh-<u>kan</u>-doe kohn ee <u>vos</u>-tree ah-<u>mee</u>-chee?)*	Are you still playing with your friends?
Seconda classe *(say-<u>cohn</u>-dah <u>klas</u>-say)*	Second Class
Settanta cinque euro *(say-<u>tan</u>-ta <u>cheen</u>-kway eh-<u>oo</u>-roe)*	Seventy-five euros
Si, nessun problema *(see, nay-<u>soon</u> proh-<u>blem</u>-ah)*	Yes, no problem
Signor *(sig-<u>nor</u>)*	Mister/Sir
Signora *(sig-<u>nor</u>-ah)*	Madame/Mrs.
Signorina *(sig-nor-<u>een</u>-ah)*	Miss

Stiamo giocando con i nostri compagni di scuola *(stee-ah-moe jee-oh-kahn-doe kon ee nos-tree kom-pag-nee dee sku-o-lah)*	We are playing with our friends from school
Subito *(soo-bee-toe)*	Immediately
Un'ora e venti minuti *(oon-ohr-ah eh ven-tee men-oo-tee)*	An hour and twenty minutes
Va bene *(vah ben-ay)*	It's OK, it's good

What are your favorite five Italian terms?

1.

2

3.

4.

5.

MORE ABOUT THE PLACES YOU VISITED IN ITALY.
→

 # ITALY

Italy is a country in southern Europe that, on a map, looks like a lady's high-heeled boot. The top of the boot touches France, Switzerland, and Austria, and the other three sides are bordered by the Mediterranean Sea. At the toe is the island of Sicily, which looks like a ball being kicked by the boot. San Marino, the oldest republic in the world, is in Italy, and Vatican City, the smallest country in the world and home of the pope, also finds itself within Italy's borders.

Italy was founded over 750 years before the birth of Christ by twin brothers Romulus and Remus. Over 60 million people live in this beautiful country and nearly 100 million tourists visit each year.

Hmmm . . .
1. Italy is known for its delicious food. Are there any Italian dishes that you and your family enjoy?

2. What was your favorite city the CLUB US crew members visited on their mission in Italy, and why?

ROME

With over four million residents, Rome is the most populated city in Italy. It is the capital of the country, and people travel from all over the world to see its historic monuments and art treasures. The earliest settlers came to Rome more than 2,700 years ago, and the city was the capital of the Roman Empire until 330 AD.

Vatican City is an independent country inside Rome's boundaries; this is the only existing example of a country within a city. Rome has sometimes been defined as the capital of two states.

Much like the rest of Italy, Rome is predominantly Roman Catholic, and the city has been an important center of religion and pilgrimage for centuries.

Hmmm . . .
1. Have you ever seen movies, cartoons, or documentaries about Rome? If so, what did you find interesting about the Italian capital?

2. The crew faced challenges and had fun in Rome. Which one of their escapades there do you remember most?

TREVI FOUNTAIN

Trevi Fountain is the largest fountain in Rome and took thirty-two years to build. Though the original fountain had been in place since 1453, construction on the current fountain began in 1730 and finished in 1762. Over two million gallons of recycled water flow through Trevi Fountain every day, and millions of tourists visit the monument annually.

In Italian, *Trevi* means "three ways," and the fountain stands at the intersection of three Roman streets. Swimming isn't allowed in the fountain and those who do so are fined. It is said that throwing a coin, over your left shoulder, into the fountain will ensure you'll return to Rome. Almost $2 million are collected every year in Trevi Fountain and given to a Catholic charity to help the poor and homeless.

Hmmm . . .
1. If you were to build a fountain like Trevi, what statues would you use in the design?

2. Giving the money collected in the fountain to help the poor and homeless is a wonderful way to make a difference. What other ways do you think the money could be used?

THE COLOSSEUM

The building of the Colosseum started around 70 AD and took ten years to complete. The 50,000 seat structure was used for gladiator contests and animal hunts, in which animals would hunt and eat prisoners, or in which gladiators would fight against animals. There were also prisoner executions and plays, and sometimes it was filled with water to fight sea battles. The Romans could enjoy these events free of charge.

Today the Colosseum is a ruin, but millions of people flock to Rome to see it every year. It's fun and spooky to take a tour of the Colosseum at night and walk through the same dark tunnels the gladiators did.

Hmmm...
1. Would you have liked to see one of the many events that took place in the Colosseum? If so, which one and why?

2. What kind of stories have you heard about the Colosseum? If you haven't heard one, make up a tale about something that could have happened there and tell it to your friends or family.

POMPEII

In 79 AD, a volcano called Mount Vesuvius erupted near Pompeii. The lava and ash that spewed from the volcano killed all of the city's residents. It all happened in one day, and what was once a thriving community was gone. The lava moved so quickly that fleeing people were quickly covered with the chemicals and died in the exact positions they were in at the time.

Before the eruption, Pompeii was a beautiful and wealthy city. Many people had vacation homes there and spent their holidays relaxing with family.

Today a visit to Pompeii is quite spectacular. The houses, stores, and restaurants are in ruin, but you can go inside and imagine what life must have been like there 2,000 years ago.

Hmmm . . .
1. What could the people of Pompeii have done to save themselves?

2. What would you be most curious to see if you had a chance to visit Pompeii?

# CAPRI

Capri, a small island, is one of the most beautiful places in Italy. Just about everything on the Amalfi Coast, and in Capri, is built into the mountainside. In most places on the Amalfi Coast, cars cannot drive up the mountain; many people must walk to the top to go home and to the bottom to go to the grocery store.

People from all over the world visit Capri for vacation in summer, but it is mostly reserved for the rich and famous. Many of the homes are villas and the stores and restaurants are expensive. The most visited attraction in Capri is the Blue Grotto. The Blue Grotto is a cave on the water that people can visit in a small open boat. The opening is very narrow and visitors must lay down in the boat to enter. Once inside, the water is so blue that it completely illuminates the cave without any light whatsoever.

Hmmm...
1. Would you like to live in a town that is built into a mountain? How would you get heavy items like furniture, refrigerators, and other household necessities to the top?

2. Would you be afraid to enter a cave like the Blue Grotto or would you welcome the experience?

 # RIMINI

Rimini is a small town of less than 150,000 inhabitants. It is always bustling with people in the street; performers working for tips; and the activity in lots of restaurants, boutiques, and bars.

The city is bordered by the Adriatic Sea and features miles and miles of beaches. During summer, Rimini is full of visitors from around Europe and the world. It is so crowded that it's almost impossible to find a spot to relax on the soft white sand, and the streets are full of cars, taxis, and especially, people.

Rimini is one of the most famous tourist destinations in Europe and has over 1,000 hotels, hundreds of vacation homes, the SeaWorld of Italy, and theme parks for all ages. The city is also proud of its culture, events, food, and wine.

Hmmm . . .
1. Rimini is a small town with friendly people. Have you visited towns like that where you live? If so, where?

2. Would you like to spend a vacation in a beach town? If so, which one?

 # VENICE

Only 55,000 people live in Venice and the population is shrinking. There are 150 canals in the city and over 400 bridges to cross them. There are no cars in Venice, and walking is the only way to get around. If people must travel long distances, they can do so by rowboat or motorboat or by taking a waterbus or water taxi. The most famous Venetian boat is a gondola and is the one we see in movies, usually with loving couples inside.

Every year the city sinks a few inches because the ground is made from mud. In spite of this, Venice is one of the most visited cities in the world.

Hmmm . . .
1. Can you imagine living in Venice? Do you think it would be fun to get everywhere you needed to go without a car?

2. Do you think people living in Venice are healthier than in other places because of all the walking they must do?

OUR NEXT adventure

Evil in Egypt

In Saqqara, where the oldest tombs in all of Egypt are found, archaeologists have discovered the burial place of King Simronwa III and his wife, Mesephia who ruled in the 5th century. The ancient leaders amassed a wealth of jewels and precious metals and buried them in their tomb along with other treasures they believed would serve them in the afterlife. Soldiers from Qumar also learned of the discovery. They have come to Egypt to rob the tomb for elureum, a metal that only existed in ancient Egypt. Obtaining the metal will allow them to build a deadly missile to destroy Borduria, the neighboring country with whom they have fought for decades.

CLUB US must stop the Qumarians from robbing the tomb of elureum and killing millions of innocent people.

Can they do it?

Evil in Egypt
(Excerpt)

Gold called Mohammed but he didn't answer. She had to make a decision.

"Since we can't reach Mohammed, we need to get to the Saqqara Pyramids in case he is there. He may be in trouble and not know it," she said.

Nikko put Saqqara Pyramids into the navigational system on his phone, and it said it was only 19 miles from town.

"We aren't far from the Giza Pyramids, maybe we can go there, and Amman can help us get to Saqqara. Let's find another taxi."

They ran outside and hailed a taxi to take them to the pyramids. When they arrived, they ran over to Amman's camel station, but he wasn't there. They saw his brother Abdul.

"Hi Abdul, remember us?" asked Eddie.

"Yes, I remember you. What do you want?" said Abdul.

"Where is Amman today?"

"He isn't here, and I'm in charge of the station. What do you need?"

Now wasn't the time to play games. They had to get to Saqqara right away.

"Abdul, there is something I have to tell you," said Gold. She didn't want to embarrass Mohammed in front of his little brother, but if she didn't, Mohammed might be hurt by the Qumarians.

Gold explained everything to Abdul, and he wasn't surprised.

"I knew something was going on, but I didn't know what it was. My brother is a good man, but if he thought he could help the people of Qumar and our mother with her cancer treatments, I can totally understand. What can we do?"

"We need to get to Saqqara as quickly as possible. Can you help us?" said Gold.

"Yes, I can. We can get there by camel in less than an hour. I only have three camels but I have lots of friends here. I will find three more, just give me a few minutes."

Abdul went around to the other stands at the Pyramids and within minutes he came back with three more camels.

"You have on the right clothes. I am going to leave the park alone and in two minutes, you follow behind me. If we leave together, it might arouse suspicion."

"OK," said Eddie.

Abdul rode towards the exit. The kids kept their eyes glued on him. As soon as he was safely out of the park, they jumped on their camels and followed. Once outside the gate, they all took off in the direction of Saqqara. . .six camels on a mission.

WITHOUT YOU THIS WOULD NOT HAVE BEEN POSSIBLE!

MY FAMILY
Each and every one of you!

MY FRIENDS
Too many to mention.

MY EDITOR
Fiona Simpson

MY PROOFREADER
Jillian Harvey

MY GRAPHIC DESIGNERS
Kate Z. Stone & Jake Naylor

MY COVER ILLUSTRATOR
Claudia Gadotti

MY SOCIAL MEDIA MANAGER
Brianna Bryson

MY CANINE CREW
Beau, Bella, Monster & Diesel

MY READERS
You!

ABOUT THE AUTHOR

More than anything, Mya Reyes loves being a mom.
Her kids have inspired her to imagine fun stories
about the amazing adventures they've experienced
in their global travels, and CLUB US is the result.

She has visited or lived in 42 countries, worked for
the United Nations UNESCO office in Paris,
gave birth to and raised Valentina and Mario in Italy,
climbed the Great Wall of China, the Leaning Tower
of Pisa, and the Giza Pyramids in Egypt.

Mya has a bachelor's degree in French Literature
and also speaks Spanish and Italian.

She hopes you'll love reading the CLUB US
series as much as she loved writing it!

DON'T MISS ALL THE CLUB US ADVENTURES!

Peril in Paris

Crisis in Cuba

Intrigue in Italy

COMING SOON!

Evil in Egypt

Mayhem in Mexico

Anguish in Australia

Menace in Morocco

Greed in Greece

Threat in Thailand

Longshot in London

Bravery in Brazil

Chaos in Canada

Terror in Tanzania